HIDDEN RAINBOWS

An utterly gripping page-turner

FAITH MARTIN

writing as

MAXINE BARRY

JOFFE BOOKS

Revised edition 2021
Joffe Books, London
www.joffebooks.com

First published in Great Britain in 2006

This book is a work of fiction. Names, characters, businesses, organizations, places and events are either the product of the author's imagination or are used fictitiously. Any resemblance to actual persons, living or dead, events or locales is entirely coincidental.
The spelling used is British English except where fidelity to the author's rendering of accent or dialect supersedes this.

Cover art by Dee Dee Book Covers

ISBN: 978-1-78931-845-6

CHAPTER ONE

Sydney

If this was Australia as it approached winter, Persis Canfield-Hope thought, then what would it be like during their summer?

As she left the Sydney Marriott Hotel and paused outside in the bright sunshine, she suddenly put out a hand against a wall to steady herself. The stone felt hot under her hand even though it was barely ten o'clock in the morning. Eventually, the familiar fluttering warning of weakness in her knees began to subside and she walked carefully to the front of the hotel, where she knew she could catch the eye of a passing taxi.

She had been in Australia only three days and she still felt as if she'd stepped into another world. Like most westerners, she'd come to the land of Oz with the usual wild misconceptions, but so far she hadn't seen a black widow spider or yet caught a glimpse of a poisonous snake. She'd seen a lizard, though, on her second day, a little green thing which had scuttled along beside her on the pavement before dropping into the gutter and down a drainage opening, like a flash of green lightning. It had at first alarmed her — being

English, a lizard was not something you found at your feet every day — but after the initial shock, it had entranced her.

A fellow dinner guest last night had informed her that her daughter, who had migrated to Cairns the previous year, actually loved the little house lizards which inhabited her country dwelling, as they were notorious fly-killers. And in a country where flies seemed to outnumber the human population by about a zillion to one, Persis had been able to understand it.

Of course, the city of Sydney must be very far removed from what she assumed life was like in the outback.

On her first day in the city she'd taken a taxi to Sydney Harbour, where she'd rather overdone things a little by taking the Sydney Harbour Explorer. This had enabled her to stop and explore not only the famous Opera House but also The Rocks, Watsons Bay, Taronga Zoo, and Darling Harbour. Consequently, she'd returned to her hotel nearly dead on her feet and ruefully reminded that she was not long out of hospital, and was supposed to be convalescing.

That experience taught her not to be too greedy with her sightseeing, so yesterday she'd spent her time far more sensibly by rationing herself to a stroll along the promenade at Bondi Beach, followed by a few hours on the sand. There she'd been careful to lather on the sun lotion and wear a big floppy hat which cast shade not only over her head but almost her entire body as well!

Now, this third morning, she paused and looked around, wondering if she should explore Hyde Park, in which case she could walk it, or perhaps take a taxi to the Amp Tower Centrepoint complex. There she'd be able to check out the observation deck and perhaps shop till she dropped in the 140 shops which her brochure confidently told her hung out at the Centrepoint Shopping Centre.

At that moment a taxi approached, making the decision for her, so she hailed it and climbed in. Since she was still not city-savvy yet, she wondered how long the journey would take and checked her purse for both Australian dollars and coins.

She didn't see a second taxi pull in behind her, or notice the man who climbed in. And she would certainly have been far more surprised than the taxi driver to hear his passenger say, in a ruefully ironic tone, 'Please, follow the cab in front.' But Persis had no reason to look out of the back window of her own cab, and so rode in ignorance towards one of the tallest observation tower in the southern hemisphere.

In the cab behind her, Dane Culver sat back and wondered where it would be this time. So far, she was behaving like any other tourist. A well-heeled one, to be sure, since she was staying at the Marriott, but then Sydney, which was as sophisticated a city as any on the planet, wasn't exactly short of wealthy visitors.

He checked his watch, knowing that if he'd been at work he'd probably be flying the company plane right about now, on his way to check out one of the mines in Queensland, which seemed to be having some sort of water seepage problem. He sighed heavily. He knew that Wally Kent, his right-hand man, was as capable of sorting it out as he was, but that didn't make him feel any less aggrieved. And the fact that he hadn't taken a holiday in over eight years didn't make him feel any less like he was playing truant.

To make matters worse, he felt a bit like one of those American private eyes tailing his 'dame' and spouting cliches like, 'Follow that cab!' All he needed now was the hat and a cigarette to dangle from his mouth, and he could be Philip Marlowe. Except that he wasn't American; he was Australian, born and bred. And this wasn't Los Angeles or New York, it was Sydney. And unlike those celebrated hard cases, he didn't enjoy stake-outs, or tailing, or watching a beautiful woman when she wasn't aware of it.

Well, OK. Spending his days watching a beautiful woman might not have been so bad, had that beautiful woman not been Persis Canfield-Hope. As it was, just the name, Canfield-Hope, was enough to set his innards clenching in disgust and send a wave of antipathy coursing through his system.

In front, Persis paid off her driver with a smile, missing the long, speculative and appreciative look he gave her. As she stepped out of the cab, her head craning up to look at the tower, she also missed spotting, yet again, her faithful shadow.

She was dressed in a simple plain white skirt and a peach blouse, and the contrast with her shoulder-length dark brown hair was striking. Not for the first time, Dane Culver found his eyes falling to her shapely legs, which were utterly bare; her feet were clad in sensible low white sandals. He could almost see the outlines of her shoulder bones as she slung her bag over her shoulder and headed for the air-conditioned coolness inside the complex, and he wondered, irritably, why it was that so many women seemed to practically starve themselves.

Persis cheerfully paid her ten-dollar entry fee for the tower and rode to the top. Dane, seeing her get into the elevator, waited for the next ride up and emerged a few minutes later. He saw her at once, of course, attached to one of the free guided tour groups. After two days of following her around he was beginning to develop his own inner radar where she was concerned. At first, he'd kept losing her in the crowds, especially on that first action-packed day. Now, he was attuned to the movement of her head, the delicate outline of her profile and the loving gaze of the sun on that rich, deep hair.

He walked to one of the high-powered binoculars and looked out at the city he knew so well. One of his properties, 'Woona Woora', was situated on the outskirts of the city amongst the other millionaire residences. It had been his mother's choice, and since he wasn't around much, he'd felt obliged to indulge her. There she felt safe and cosseted with her bridge-playing friends all living nearby, and with home visits from masseurs, manicurists, hair stylists, and who the hell knew what else.

Dane, when he wasn't abroad promoting the sales of Culver Opals, was mostly out at their various mines or staying in his private town house overlooking Darling Harbour.

He glanced around, saw that he'd momentarily lost her, and walked the circular platform until she was once again in sight. As he watched, she walked to the railing and leaned on it. There was nothing unusual in that, of course — many people were doing the same thing, exclaiming in languages ranging from German to Thai, about the wonderful view. But the English girl didn't seem to be looking at the panorama in front of her. What's more, her grip on the railing was so tight, he could see that her knuckles were gleaming white with tension. Was she afraid of heights? His lips tightened as he took an instinctive half-step towards her. What the hell was she doing up here if she was afraid of heights? Unless she was trying to conquer her fear. But no, she was straightening up now and looking around her without a qualm.

As she turned towards him, he moved back and looked away, but not before glimpsing the pallor of her face.

Persis reached into her bag and removed a moistened tissue, rubbing it over her forehead and cheeks. That had been a nasty moment. Even now, months after she'd first started feeling ill, and nearly a month since leaving hospital, those sudden attacks of weakness could overtake her without warning.

It began as a buzzing in the head, quickly followed by the distressing feeling that, no matter how much she breathed in, not enough air was getting to her lungs. Depending on how bad the attack was, and how long it lasted, her hands could begin to shake and sometimes, worst of all, her legs would fail her. But now the light-headedness had passed and she was breathing normally.

She'd decided long ago, when the doctors and consultants and specialists could make no firm diagnosis, that she couldn't let herself be sucked into the trap of thinking of herself as an invalid. Whatever virus it was that had laid her low so unexpectedly last year, she'd come to realize that she couldn't live her life always scared to go out in case of an attack. True, she'd been forced to give up work for a while, but luckily Carole Vaughan, her business partner and fellow gallery owner, had been more than understanding.

Their gallery in Woodstock was a thriving concern, but Carole's forte had always been in manning the shop, making sales, and generally charming the tourist-cum-art-lover who flocked to Woodstock every year into parting with their money, whereas it had always been Persis's job to find the stock and cultivate or discover local talent. She also used her contacts from her days studying art history at St Bede's College in Oxford to help lure wealthy customers to the gallery's door.

Since the gallery always had stock in hand, she could afford to take up to a year off to recover from this damned illness — whatever it was. But that didn't mean that Persis intended to let it beat her. In fact, she was sure she almost had it licked. Just four months ago, she'd needed oxygen, drugs and hospitalization. Now, apart from the prescription drugs and regular visits to her doctor, she was almost back to normal. Well, nearly. She still felt tired sometimes, but nowhere near as depleted and exhausted as she had felt previously.

Now, as she looked out over the 360-degree view of the city, harbour, and over to the Blue Mountains and Wollongong, she felt herself smiling. Truly, this trip represented light at the end of the tunnel. Her doctors wouldn't have let her take the journey if they'd thought otherwise. And her mother certainly wouldn't have encouraged her to come if *she'd* had any doubts either.

Straightening her shoulders both physically and metaphorically, she turned and took the elevator back down. For a while she window-shopped, recognizing the familiar and lingering over the new. She eyed a stuffed koala for some time, wondering if she could possibly buy it. Her mother might adore it, but she was somewhat reluctant to buy such an obvious gift. No, she'd wait. With the long train journey starting tomorrow, and with all those stops along the way to Perth, she was bound to find something a little more out of the way and authentically Australian to take back home.

Or at least, she hoped so.

With a smile for the unquestionably cute stuffed koala, she slowly meandered away, eventually fetching up at an intimate little café-cum-restaurant. She took a table by some leafy ferns, sitting at a ninety-degree angle to the window and the view of the city. She ordered a mixed fruit drink, awash with ice, and a slice of kiwi-fruit tart.

Two tables away, Dane ordered a Foster's and watched her broodingly. He was definitely not happy. And not just because he was being forced to play such an absurd role, either. As he watched the waiter place her order in front of her, and saw her lift her face to smile her thanks, he was struck, not for the first time, by how wrong everything felt.

Which was, when you thought about it, absurd. Everything should seem so right, given the way things had worked out.

Disaster had struck only last month, causing him to drop everything and fly out to Perth. There, he'd found things were about as bad as they could be, and had had no choice but to bring the Canfield-Hope situation under control once and for all. For decades, first his grandfather, then his father, had let the situation slide. Perhaps they hadn't wanted to face litigation, or the possibility of a family scandal. Perhaps they'd simply been too damned gentlemanly — who could tell? Whatever the reason, with the death of his father last year, and the phone call from Perth last month, it had fallen to Dane to sort things out once and for all.

And only one result would do.

So he'd hired a reputable private enquiry agency to give him a detailed background check on the Canfield-Hope family, and had begun to organize his diary for a prolonged and reluctant stay in Britain. When the agency had told him that not only were the Canfield-Hopes reduced to only eight members, but that one of them was actually booked to fly into Sydney in three weeks' time, it had sounded like manna from heaven. The mountain coming to Mohammed, in fact.

Dane had gratefully postponed his trip to the UK and now he was waiting to see what would happen next. He somehow didn't think that it could possibly be a coincidence that a Canfield-Hope should come to Australia for a holiday just when a certain event was happening in Perth. Oh no.

From what little he'd been able to learn about the outrageous stunt the Canfield-Hopes had perpetrated against his own family between the two world wars, he knew enough to know that where the Canfield-Hopes were concerned, it paid to wear full body armour. All the better to protect your back from the inevitable stealthy knife which would try to slip in under your ribs.

So when he'd been in place at the airport three nights ago (with a helpful airport official generously bribed to point out a certain passenger at passport control), Dane had felt if not happy then at least firmly in control. For once, the Culvers were waiting for them. Ready and prepared.

However, his first sight of Persis Canfield-Hope had been a bit of a shock. Not that he'd been naive enough to think that she would look like Cruella de Vil, or even a vamp the likes of which *Dynasty* and *Dallas* had portrayed back in the eighties. But he had expected a certain . . . hardness to be detectable. A certain shallowness; a sharp-eyed, cold-hearted look which depicted a woman on the make. A gold-digger, descended from a line of gold-diggers.

But although the woman who'd got off the plane had been as well dressed as he'd expected, with the usual designer luggage to match, nothing else about her fitted the image in his mind.

Perhaps it was the obvious exhaustion which softened her features and widened her big, light-coloured eyes that disconcerted him. Perhaps it was her English pallor, or the whippet-leanness of her figure, which leant her a certain fragility. Whatever it was, after two days of following her about as she played tourist, he was still aware of that same feeling of wrongness plaguing him.

For a start, just why was she playing the wide-eyed visitor so industriously in the first place? Why, for Pete's sake, had she booked herself on a tedious coast-to-coast trip on the train? Why did she not just simply fly straight into Perth and do whatever the hell it was that she'd come to Australia to do?

And he could guess what that was all right.

Threaten them, perhaps, if there should be any 'unpleasantness'. Hint around about going to the papers and causing a family scandal.

And she could do it too, Dane thought grimly, gritting his teeth as his beer arrived, and then having to loosen his jaw before he could take a long cold swallow straight from the bottle. That was the real crux of the trouble: if he didn't play this right, she could cause one hell of a stink.

For himself, and the personal consequences, Dane didn't give a hoot. After all, the genesis of the whole sordid, miserable affair had begun between the two wars, decades before he'd even been born.

But his mother would be mortified. And, worse still, the situation in Perth would be made unendurable. What's more, Dane knew that the blow to Culver Mines, and Culver Opals in particular, could be far more damaging. Financially damaging. The stock market was so damned skittish nowadays.

Dane scowled, unaware that he was staring at Persis Canfield-Hope with laser-like intensity.

Persis, sipping her juice and shivering just slightly in the highly air-conditioned room, suddenly felt the fine hairs on the nape of her neck rise up. A moment later a certain knot formed in her back just between her shoulder blades and told her that she was being watched. An animal instinct, as old as evolution, was coming to her aid, ignoring the fact that she was ensconced in a very civilized restaurant in the middle of a big bustling city. She might as well have been a deer in an African watering hole, so loud and clear was the message.

A predator is watching you.

Slowly, carefully, she put her glass down. Leaning forward, and under the guise of drawing her plate of kiwi-fruit tart towards her, she casually looked around.

A mother with twins sitting opposite her was far too busy trying to stop one of the little girls from dripping ice cream down the front of her dress to be interested in her. A waiter was clearing a table to her right, but although she caught him casting her the usual look of admiration, she knew it wasn't him that had caused her unease. At twenty-five, Persis was used to men watching her like *that*.

She reached for her dessert fork, her eyes moving on around the room. And then she saw him. He was sitting a few tables away in a dark corner, and was lifting a bottle of beer up to his mouth. He was dressed in dark slacks and a plain white shirt. The artificial lighting in the back of the room shone on his hair, highlighting reddish and sandy-coloured depths in his mostly nut-brown hair, which was very thick and cut short but stylishly. For some reason the sight of it made her fingertips tingle, as if in anticipation of the feel of it — the warmth of his scalp contrasting against the coolness of the silken strands.

She took a quick breath, telling herself to look away, but seemed unable to do so.

His skin, she realized at once and even from a distance, was typical of that of an Australian male used to working outdoors. In Europe, she knew, a lot of people tended to turn a reddish bronze, even those who worked outdoors all the time, like farmers and construction workers. But in Australia, people who lived in perpetual sun went a colour all of their own. This man had skin like that. Healthy. Tough. As if carved from rock.

From where she was sitting, she couldn't see the colour of his eyes, only make out that they were light, in the tan of his face. And they were staring at her like . . . well . . . like a lion watched a gazelle.

Dane, unexpectedly finding himself meeting her eyes, cursed mentally, and casually looked away.

Persis, for some reason that she couldn't quite understand, felt herself blushing. As if *she* was the one who'd committed some sort of faux pas.

She quickly turned her attention back to her tart, which she knew she would no longer be able to eat. Guiltily she pushed it away, even though she'd promised both her mother and doctor that she'd try to put back on some much-needed weight.

She pushed her half-finished drink away also, and got up. She would go back to the hotel and take a nap. After that, she'd find a nice restaurant somewhere and then have an early night. Although she didn't have to catch the train until nearly three o'clock tomorrow afternoon, she still had to re-pack, and she wanted to take some of the time tomorrow morning to say a final goodbye to Sydney. Although it was perhaps the most famous of the Australian cities, and was certainly home to a vast number of Australia's citizens, she was anxious to see something more of the country.

That was one of the two reasons why she'd decided to take the train, coast to coast, from Sydney to Perth in the first place. The second reason rested snugly in her handbag. She could even feel the comforting bulk of her grandmother's diary as it rested on her hip.

She'd started to read it in hospital, after her mother had discovered it amongst some old things in the attic. Knowing her daughter's romantic streak, plus her interest in the grandmother that she'd never met, Sara Canfield-Hope had taken it in for her to peruse, as a way to help pass the long, lonely hospital hours.

It had worked only too well, for Persis had quickly become fascinated by the account of the trip to Australia her grandmother had taken in the spring of 1938. She, too, had gone coast to coast, and it was then that the germ of the idea of coming to Australia had taken hold. Of course, she knew that the Australia of 1938 would bear no comparison to the country of the brave new millennium, but then, it was in the changes, as well as in the things that stayed the same, where the interest would lie.

Now, Persis slipped the diary out of her bag and glanced at it for a moment, the man at the other table all but forgotten. Some of the passages in her grandmother's diary had been fascinating and romantic. Others were downright mysterious. In places, her ancestor had even gone into a kind of shorthand which made no sense to her. But studying it during that long month in the John Radcliffe Hospital, Persis had begun to get ideas. Fascinating, wonderful ideas. If true.

And perhaps, as she followed in her grandmother's footsteps, she'd be given the chance to find out. Maybe even the mystery surrounding the enigmatic Iris that her grandmother mentioned in the pages of her journal would be uncovered? She smiled gently. She hoped so.

Dane's eyes sharpened at the sight of the old book in her hand. He too was on his feet and already walking towards her, caught out by her sudden change of mind. Instead of leaving the table, as he'd expected, she'd reached into her bag instead, giving him a clear view of what she was holding. He could see, from the yellowed pages, that it was old, and although her hand covered most of it, the gold-leafed first three letters, 'DIA', told him that she was holding a diary.

An old diary.

He felt his hands clench into fists as he wondered whose it was. And, more importantly, what it said. To some extent he was still working blind. Oh, he knew basically what had happened all those years ago and just what the Canfield-Hopes had done; or rather, what one particular woman had done. But the details were sparse. Sketchy. He had only boyhood memories of the stories his father had told him about the old days, and some of his grandfather's letters, to guide him. But instinct told him that the diary in Persis Canfield-Hope's hand would answer a lot more questions for him.

Dammit, he had to get his hands on it. Copy it, maybe. But first, he'd have to play the role of thief. Renewed anger washed over him. That he should be reduced to this!

Persis put the diary back in her bag, unaware that the predator was only a few steps away now, and left the table. As she moved away, however, she felt her knees suddenly give their warning flutter, and felt herself misstep. She lurched, instinctively reaching out to grab hold of something. Anything.

Her head spun.

Not now, she thought in dismay, or maybe even whispered aloud.

Dane saw her stumble and reach out, noticed the sudden whiteness of her face and the panicked look that leapt into her eyes, and moved fast. Within a second, he had his arm around her.

Persis went from a hideously helpless feeling of groping at nothing but air, to suddenly finding herself supported. Solid, warm, strong arms held her upright.

She looked up and began to smile.

Grey, Dane thought. Her eyes are grey. Big, beautiful grey eyes. And suddenly realized that he'd been wondering about the colour of her eyes ever since he'd first seen her.

Green, Persis thought. His eyes are green. Not emerald, but something more natural. Meadow green.

'I'm sorry,' she found herself murmuring. 'I just . . . slipped.'

Dane managed to smile and nodded curtly. 'All right now?' he asked gruffly, and Persis, sensing that he was anxious to get away, nodded quickly, her chin coming up, fighting fit.

'Yes, thank you,' she said coolly. 'Perfectly.'

Dane nodded and walked away. But it was one of the hardest things he'd ever done.

He'd known that she was beautiful, of course. But he'd never been close enough before to see just *how* beautiful. And those eyes. So unexpected. He'd never thought of grey eyes as beautiful before. And her perfume had been intoxicating — something light and tangy, reminding him of orange blossoms. He could still smell it now, haunting his senses. No doubt it would haunt his dreams too. His palms could still feel the residual heat of her skin, and where the slight rounded pressure of her breast had pressed against his forearm, a pulse throbbed.

When he walked outside, he was breathing hard. He shook his head, telling himself to forget it. He was a man and she was beautiful. It meant nothing. He was between girlfriends at the moment, that was all. It wouldn't take him long to find another bed partner, then such purely physical reflexes wouldn't bother him.

He certainly wasn't going to let it get in the way of what he had to do.

Persis, leaving the shopping centre by another door, took a taxi back to her hotel, firmly trying to forget the predator with green eyes. After all, she was hardly likely to see him again, was she? It had just been one of those funny little unsettling moments which life could throw at you sometimes. A mere second or two of the unusual, the exotic and the unknown amid a sea of routine and the familiar.

But just for a moment there . . .

No. She shook her head firmly. No. Definitely not.

* * *

Back at his townhouse, Dane Culver called a now-familiar number in Perth.

'Hello, it's me. Yes, I've seen her. We'll be in Perth in less than two weeks. Don't worry. By then it'll all be sorted.' He waited, listened with pity and a sense of sad frustration as the woman on the end of the line spoke haltingly, then nodded. 'Yes,' he said softly. 'I will. I promise.'

And Dane Culver was a man who always kept his promises. He hung up and walked to the windows, looking out over the harbour.

'The Canfield-Hopes won't get away with it this time,' he said softly.

CHAPTER TWO

The Indian Pacific *and Bathurst*

Persis arrived at the Sydney terminal the next day well in time, and to while away the time, began reading the brochure about the train she was about to take. Its emblem, she noted, was a wedge-tailed eagle, the biggest in Australia and steeped in the Dreamtime legends of the Pitjantjatjara people. Fascinated, she read on, learning how the eagle, called Waluwara, lived in the Musgrave Ranges and shared his camp with his mate, a pink cockatoo called Tukalili, and with a crow-man called Kanga and his wife. One day, after Waluwara returned from a long hunting flight, a fight broke out in which his mate and the crow-man's wife were killed. The crow-man, in revenge, killed Waluwara with his boomerang and the great eagle's spirit soared into the sky where he became the Southern Cross.

Letting the brochure fall into her lap, Persis sighed, enchanted by this glimpse into Aboriginal myth. Tonight, she knew, she'd look out of her cabin window and hope to spot the Southern Cross in the sky. Then she sighed and returned to the brochure to check up on much more practical matters, quickly finding that her first-class single cabin would suit her admirably. Although tiny, it had a comfortable lounge chair (which at night converted into a single bed), as well as a toilet and washbasin, fresh towels, a small wardrobe, vanity mirror and three-pin power point. There was also a foldaway table and reading lamp. Showers, she was happy to note, were located at the end of each car. There were, she was less happy to note, eighteen compartments to a car, but then, since she was breaking up the journey at nearly every stage, she wouldn't be spending too much time on board in one stretch. And although the journey from Sydney to Perth was sixty-four hours, her first stop in Bathurst was only five and a half hours away.

But Persis was not the only one to be impressed by the train itself, once she had boarded.

Rayne Fletcher, unpacking just the bare essentials in her own first-class cabin, was also impressed, but far more concerned about whether or not she should change before going to the lounge car which, she assumed, would be treated by most passengers as the local pub! Normally she wouldn't bother, for the simple white slacks and ice-blue blouse she was wearing were still fresh and suited her five-feet four-inch frame admirably. Especially since her fair hair was short and curly, and her eyes almost the exact same shade of blue as the blouse.

But Avery McLeod would almost certainly venture into the lounge car sooner or later and it was imperative that she attract his attention. With no idea just how much time she had before things started moving back home in the UK, there was no time for subtlety. She needed to make contact and, if at all possible, get close enough to him to see if she could find out just what he was up to. So she extracted a short white cocktail dress with a feminine scalloped hem which hung just above her knees. She carefully smoothed on sheer, white-tinged silk stockings and a pair of strappy gold shoes. The V-shaped neckline framed a simple gold and pearl drop pendant to perfection and she added a touch of mascara and silver-blue eyeshadow to bring out the startling effect of her eyes. Luckily, her short curly hair, cut in a delightful gamine style to frame her heart-shaped face, needed little attention, and she simply combed and fluffed it.

She gave a mew of surprise as the train suddenly gave a tiny lurch, and she realized they were off. She could imagine passengers leaning out of the window, waving goodbye to friends, and smiled whimsically. Well, there was no one she had to wave goodbye to, since all her friends were half a world away back in England. Besides, she was here to do a job of work and not, as some of her more envious colleagues back at Reut, Cole and Phipps had assumed, to indulge in a glorified holiday. In fact, just last week, Matt Cole, the senior partner, had called her into his office and all but laid it on the line. The firm was looking to appoint another partner after Wilhelm Reut had retired last year, and they didn't particularly want to go outside. In fact, he'd told her frankly, the race was on between her and Pete Smithfield, who was Gary Phipps's first choice.

'But if you can get this Cloud Nine fiasco sorted out, Rayne, I think I can safely say it'll mean your promotion is in the bag.' Even now, with a flush of pleasure, Rayne could hear him saying this, his level brown gaze resting on her thoughtfully.

Well, she was not going to blow it, Rayne thought determinedly, checking her appearance one more time and adding a dash of Yves St Laurent's 'Rive Gauche' behind her ears and on her wrists. Closing and locking her cabin door, she made her way, swaying slightly, towards the lounge car. Time to let battle commence.

She'd worked too long and too hard, and had had to fight all sorts of male prejudice which dominated her career choice, to get where she was today. And she intended to go higher. Much higher.

* * *

Because of the early arrival in Bathurst, the dining car was opening early, and by five o'clock the lounge car, which could comfortably seat up to fifty, was beginning to fill with people out to enjoy a pre-dinner aperitif.

So far, Rayne had had to fight off the amorous attentions of several men, much to the stewards' amusement. She supposed, in a way, she was asking for it, dressed to kill and sitting all alone. In fact, she hoped it would be just this little-girl-lost aspect which would attract Avery McLeod — if he ever showed. Always fair-minded, she knew she couldn't really blame lone males for trying it on. It was just annoying, especially when she was working.

She ordered her second White Russian and was sipping it sparingly when she suddenly saw him. Although she'd seen his photograph (she'd read and reread the huge dossier her firm had built up on him) she felt herself stiffening, mainly because the photographs hardly did him justice. Some men, she knew, were flattered by a camera. Others, as in this case, loved them not at all. So instead of being confronted by the average-looking individual she'd expected, Rayne found herself watching one of the most attractive men she'd ever encountered. As he walked to the bar, she expertly ran her eye over him, guessing his height at just over five feet ten. Not too tall for someone her size, she found herself thinking, then just as automatically pushed the thought aside. His hair, far from being the indifferent mousy brown of his photograph, was a rich, deep, toffee colour, and when he accepted his beer and turned to glance around for a spare table, she just knew his eyes were going to be the deep, rich brown of dark chocolate.

They were, and fastened on her at once, and not only because she was occupying one of the few tables left available which had any room. She smiled politely, the sort of smile which acknowledged his dilemma and assented, in a very correct and British way, to his joining her. Just because she had a table and a spare chair, and manners dictated it. Naturally.

Avery McLeod made no attempt to hide the look which leapt, as naturally as breathing, into his eyes. She was gorgeous. Petite, blonde, and had the biggest pair of pale blue eyes anywhere. More than a man, far from home and doomed to a long and probably tedious train journey, could possibly hope for.

As he walked towards her Rayne noted with a twinge of alarm the lean agility of his body, coupled with a tension which was strictly sexual. Instantly, she felt herself responding to his charisma and she mentally shook her head. No way, girl! But it would be nice. And, as he came closer and she saw the questioning fire in his eyes, and felt her own libido answering joyously back, she realized just how nice it would probably be.

It was such a pity that he was a crook.

'Do you mind?' he asked politely, just in case he'd read the signals wrong, and indicated the chair and his drink. Rayne upped the wattage of her smile a few notches and moved her own drink a little to one side.

'No, please,' she said, indicating the chair.

Rituals over, Avery sat slowly down, letting his eyes fall to her legs as he did so and then slowly bringing them back up to her face. She was, he guessed, about twenty-five or so, certainly no older. And no wedding ring. 'Did I detect a fellow British accent?' he asked, and Rayne laughed.

'Guilty as charged,' she admitted brightly. And, thrusting out her hand added simply, 'Rayne Fletcher.'

Avery hastily took her hand. 'Avery McLeod,' he said, liking a woman who could just straightforwardly introduce herself like that. With no artifice and no coyness.

Rayne grinned wider, knowing that it gave her gamine face an even greater charm. She was perfectly willing to use his obvious attraction to her and felt only a meagre measure of guilt at doing so. After all, it was her job. And it wasn't as if he was some innocent babe in the woods, was it?

'So, you're here on holiday?' Avery asked and Rayne sighed. She wished!

'Oh yes,' she lied glibly. 'I've always wanted to see Australia. And by train seemed the best way of doing it.' She leaned over and took a sip of her drink, careful to let it wet her lips. 'I'm going all the way,' she added, utterly deadpan.

Avery felt the jolt of the sexual double entendre hit him squarely in the solar plexus and wondered what she'd do if he said, 'I'll bet you are,' as he instinctively wanted to. He even had the idea that this intriguing little thing would not only take it in her stride but toss the ball right back at him.

But he wasn't sure that he wanted to play that game. Not just yet.

'Perth is supposed to be nice,' he said diplomatically, and saw her eyes widen and a reluctant smile tug at her lips. Was that respect he saw dance fleetingly in and out of those eyes?

'So I've been told,' Rayne said.

Avery reluctantly glanced at his watch. To cover her instant alarm, she quipped lightly, 'Going somewhere?' and glanced pointedly at the scenery speeding by, the never-ending sparse earth, dazzling sky and the watchful Blue Mountains. Avery looked too, and laughed.

'No. But I am getting off at Bathurst,' he said, with a regret which didn't have to be faked.

'Really? So am I,' Rayne lied instantly. Although in truth she'd made no specific plans as to her itinerary, simply because she didn't know what Avery McLeod himself had planned. But one thing was for sure — wherever he went she was going to follow.

He looked at her quickly, with genuine and happy surprise and not the least hint of suspicion. To keep it that way, she glanced once more out of the window at the passing eucalyptus and instantly thought of something normal to say. 'I suppose we'll get to see some kangaroos sometime?'

Avery laughed. 'They tell me Australia is full of them. Although around here it's more likely to be brush-tailed rock wallabies. And if you're not of a nervous disposition, grey-headed fruit bats and eastern water rats.'

Rayne blinked. 'Huh?' she said bluntly, batting her eyelashes shamelessly.

'And if you're interested in birds,' Avery continued, knowing full damn well what she was doing but willing to oblige her by showing off, 'there are the usual kookaburras and parrots, but with honeyeaters thrown in.'

'You a zoologist by any chance?' she asked, and Avery laughed.

'No. I studied up on it before I came.' In fact, he'd studied up on a lot of things before coming to check out things here. After all, he could hardly offer his Cloud Nine customers a coast-to-coast trip through Australia unless he had done his homework first. 'I own a travel company,' he explained, seeing her widen her eyes at him questioningly. 'We specialize in the more unusual kind of holidays. I was thinking of adding a Sydney to Perth trip by train as another option, but . . .' He shrugged graphically, and Rayne, who knew it all already, laughed.

'But you had to check it out first, just to see if it was up to your standard. Meaning, coming all the way here yourself, no doubt in a first-class cabin, and seeing the sights on offer,' she finished for him, nodding her head. 'You poor baby.'

Avery grinned. 'Last time it was checking out a backpacking route across Nepal. The Abominable Snowman nearly got me.'

Rayne's eyes twinkled. 'Big brave you. Compared to that, this must be a bit tame,' she said, indicating the train. 'Don't tell me — I'll bet you've got all the train's particulars off by heart too. What is it with men and machinery?'

Avery grinned. 'Oh, let's see. It's 498 metres in length with 130 doors. The locomotives are National Rail NRCs, and its average speed is 85 kilometres an hour. First class accommodates 88, holiday class 64 and coach class 124. There are eighteen full-time staff, and sixteen drivers who are regularly changed. The journey time—'

'Stop it,' Rayne admonished sharply. 'You're making my head spin.' Just then a steward announced that the dining car was open for any passengers leaving them at Bathurst.

Avery met her glance. 'You'll dine with me?' he asked, already knowing the answer.

'Of course I will,' Rayne said promptly. Just let wild horses try and stop her!

She followed him to the dining car, doing quick mental calculations. Thanks to her company, which was one of the biggest and richest insurance companies in their area of expertise, she had been given a more or less no-holes-barred expense account. And considering what they'd have to pay up if Avery McLeod's fraudulent and downright criminal claim had to be met, Rayne was not surprised they'd been so generous with the investigator assigned to the case. So getting a hotel in Bathurst wouldn't be a problem.

Avery opened the door for her and ushered her into the Queen Adelaide restaurant. As she swept by him, with a toss of her glossy blonde curls, he anticipated a very lively few hours.

Rayne smiled as he pulled back a chair for her and expected to be nailing his hide to the wall long before they reached Perth.

* * *

Persis alighted at Bathurst, a porter eagerly taking her bags for her and offering to secure a taxi. She hoped, with a pang, that she didn't still look as if a mere puff of wind would blow her over, but she needn't have worried. The porter was far more taken with her beauty than her undeniable air of fragility.

There were a few moments of hectic activity as passengers disembarked and some new ones climbed aboard. In the rush and crowd, Persis suddenly noticed one head, a fine, dark head, standing out from all the others. The man must have been well over six feet tall to enable him to tower above the others as he did, and for a moment, as he turned to glance at the exit, she saw his profile . . . and felt the ground beneath her feet move, giving her the weird feeling of standing on air.

Dane Culver, sensing her proximity like a metal filing being drawn to a magnet, suddenly turned sharply and, over the sea of people, found himself suddenly staring at her.

Persis felt her heart lift. It was him. The predator. But with the rush of unexpected joy came also a quick, dampening wave of warning. This was not good.

Oh, it was not the amazing coincidence of seeing him again which worried her so much. After all, coincidences happened all the time. But the fact that it should affect her so much worried her. She'd literally spoken a few words to this man, nothing more. Seen him, literally, only once before. And yet here she was, feeling so glad to see him again. It was illogical. Unreasonable. And the last time she'd felt like this had been when she was with Rob.

Rob, the man she'd almost married. Rob, the man who'd left her. And she simply was not going to go through that again. Not again. Not now that she'd finally fought free of all that pain and misery.

As Dane took the first of his steps towards her, Persis turned and fled. It wasn't very discreet. There could be no hiding the fact that she'd seen him. In fact, there was something almost panic-stricken about it.

Grimly, as he watched her familiar figurehead for the exit, he wondered if she'd finally realized who he was. And if so, how had she found out and what did she plan on doing about it? He knew that he would have to find out. And quickly.

* * *

As she'd thought, Rayne had no trouble finding a hotel — or in this case, the Atlas Motel — and booking in for the night. She told the clerk she might be staying on another night, since she had no way of knowing how long Avery intended on staying, and after a quick bath and change of clothes into a long scarlet dress of pure silk, quickly checked the brochures for her best chance of relocating her quarry.

They'd said goodbye at the train station and she'd been quick to leave first. After all, she couldn't make it too obvious that she intended to stick to him like glue.

The city, she quickly realized, had a typical goldrush history behind it, but nowadays relied on farm stays, bush walking, shopping, festivals and the world-famous Mount Panorama to attract visitors. Luckily for her the late-night dining choice wasn't all that huge, and after half an hour or so she succeeded in tracking him down to the Ziegler's Café, a relaxed, rather stylish and innovative place. He was seated at a table in a pleasantly leafy courtyard, and Rayne was careful to walk past his table. The waiter following on behind her watched her derrière rather obviously.

'Rayne Fletcher, as I live and breathe,' he said, watching her spin around and her face light up. Now that was a welcoming sight for any man.

'Avery McLeod, zoologist,' she said, puzzling the waiter, who realized, with a sigh, that the lady wouldn't be dining alone after all. Within moments she was seated, and had ordered a light snack.

Avery, dressed in a cool white evening shirt and cinnamon-coloured slacks, leaned his elbows on the table and cupped his chin in one palm, watching her blatantly.

'Are you following me?' he teased, unknowingly making her heart stand still for an uncomfortable moment.

'You wish!' she shot back, recovering her aplomb in a nanosecond. 'It's just that this is the classiest place in town, and as I'm a classy lady — *voila*!' She spread her hands wide in a telling, vampish gesture.

'*Voila*, indeed,' he said. But she was right. She was the most classy lady he'd met in a long time and she knew it. And what was wrong with that? Avery liked confident women. Unlike most men, they didn't frighten him, or even unnerve him. And why should they? He'd grown up on a working-class estate in the Midlands and now was joint owner of a million-pound business. To accomplish that, he had to have his own fair share of confidence and self-esteem. Shrinking violets only puzzled him.

'In fact, I've been thinking,' he said, almost as if he'd been speaking aloud and was merely following on a conversation which had been going on for hours.

Rayne blinked outlandishly. 'No! Did it hurt?'

'Cheeky wench,' he said. 'No, seriously. I'm here to check out this coast-to-coast trip to see if it would make a good break for my customers, right?'

'Hence checking out all the good and classy places to go?' she agreed, waving a hand to indicate the café.

'Exactly. But what I really need is another eye. The eye of someone who's actually already here on holiday. The eye of someone who's out to have a good time, not work, like me. What better way is there to find out where the good times really are to be had than to get a second opinion?'

Rayne could have leapt up and kissed him. Literally. Here she'd been, racking her brains to come up with a reason to stay close by his side without him getting suspicious, and here he was offering it to her on a plate.

What a lovely man.

It really *was* such a pity that he was a crook.

'You mean you want me to act as your guinea pig?' she asked, raising an eyebrow in scandalized shock, ruining her high, outraged tone somewhat by accompanying it with an impish grin. 'Why didn't you just say so? And here I was, thinking you were a man with nefarious purposes in mind.'

Avery ogled her like a villain from a Victorian melodrama. 'Oh, I have those in mind too,' he assured her.

'Oh. That's all right then,' Rayne said, mollified.

* * *

The next morning Rayne dressed early and fast, wishing she'd been booked into the same place as her mark. Unfortunately, he'd already got rooms at the Panorama City Hotel but next time she'd find out where he was staying first, even if she had to follow him around like a hound dog.

They met for breakfast at his place, and she groaned as he listed the attractions on offer, which ranged from the Abercrombie Caves, to the Bathurst Sheep and Cattle Drome, to the Australian Fossil and Mineral Museum. And he was serious.

For a second, Rayne felt a moment of misgiving. Why was a man who was planning on raiding his corporation's finances and swindling an insurance company out of half a million, before swanning off to the Bahamas, so intent on working so hard? It wasn't as if Cloud Nine Holidays was going to survive and actually offer an Australian holiday, was it?

Then she shrugged the thought aside. He was probably just being clever. A man with his nous must know that his insurance company wouldn't take such a large and highly suspicious claim lying down. They'd be bound to investigate. So he was just playing the role of hard-working owner, just in case anyone was watching. So she'd go along with him.

Concurring with him that sheep and cattle probably wouldn't be a first-class travel seeker's primary choice, she agreed to accompany him to the Mount Panorama Winery, followed by a quick trip to the Historical Museum and thence to check out Bowenfels Cashmeres.

They were scheduled to catch the train for Broken Hill at 7.30 that night. 'We have to keep to a two-week schedule,' he explained. 'Given that customers would probably like to spend a few days in Sydney and Perth either end, we only have nine days or so to complete the whole trip.'

As they set off arm in arm, Rayne Fletcher was feeling happy and rather proud of herself. But she really should have remembered the old adage about pride and what it usually preceded.

Avery McLeod was not the kind of man to play the fool for anybody. Not even a saucy, beautiful, hard-as-nails blonde.

* * *

Persis Canfield-Hope might not have been feeling so happy (and certainly nowhere near as cocky) as Rayne Fletcher, but she was feeling more relaxed.

After an early night and a long sleep she felt much better, and a light breakfast had set her up for the day. She rather thought, uneasily, that she had dreamed of 'the predator' during the night, but since she hardly ever remembered her dreams, she couldn't be sure. Only a feeling of flushed excitement, mixed with something warm and somehow dangerous, remained with her the next morning to give her any hint.

Now she was sat in the dappled shade of a big unknown tree at Machattie Park. She'd walked past and admired the caretaker's cottage and the bandstand, and had thrown a coin into Crago Fountain, making her wish. Other fountains now danced their tuneful songs all around her, and the begonia house beckoned for later on. Right now, though, she was content simply to sit in the dappled sunlight and read her grandmother's diary.

She turned to one of her favourite passages.

Walter C. told me today of his wife. There was such pain in his eyes, and obvious shame, that I could not answer him as angrily as I knew I should have. Walter has only to look at me from that dear, craggy, rather ugly face, and I know I am lost. But oh, a wife!

Persis sighed and glanced around her, staring in surprise at a parrot perched on a nearby picnic table. Of course, parrots, galahs and all sorts of coloured lorikeets were as common over here as house sparrows were in Britain. But how strange to see cockatoos roaming wild!

She glanced back at the diary, trying to imagine being in her grandmother's shoes. An Englishwoman far from home, meeting and falling in love with her darling 'Walter C', as she always referred to him. A man older than herself, wise and knowledgeable. Persis could almost feel the love her grandmother had felt for her lover wafting off the pages, which were themselves decades old. To travel so far and meet the love of her life, only to discover he was married! Persis wasn't sure what she'd have done in the same situation. The fact that her grandmother hadn't broken off the relationship was obvious. Later . . .

A shadow fell across the diary and she looked up, expecting to see a park keeper, perhaps, or a fellow seeker of shade. But she supposed, in some secret part of her, that she'd always known it would be him, for when she met his green eyes she didn't feel in the least surprised.

'Hello again,' he said simply. 'We've met, haven't we?'

Persis nodded. 'In Sydney. And I saw you at the station yesterday.' He knew all this. She knew he did, and he knew she knew.

Dane nodded and took the seat next to her. She was aware, only too well aware, of his long length as he sat beside her. He was built like a wolf, all wiry strength, and with the kind of physical toughness which would let him go on for ever, without ever getting tired. Beside him, she felt even weaker and more physically puny than usual. But instead of it frustrating her, as it had done before, something warm and melting seemed to be seeping into her instead, making her feel things she hadn't felt in a long, long time. She took a slow, deep breath and told herself not to panic.

So she was attracted to him. That was normal. It was inevitable that her body, after a long illness, and her psyche, after the blow Rob had dealt it, would both recover enough to get back to normal. It didn't mean she had to react. She could just get up and walk away.

'My name's Dane Culver,' the predator said, watching her face closely. And saw nothing. Not a flicker of recognition. No paling of the skin, no widening of the eyes.

'Persis Canfield-Hope,' she said, smiling shyly.

Dane nodded. So, she didn't know who he was. She might, of course, have been a superb actress, but he didn't think so. So why had she fled from him so obviously back at the train station? It was an intriguing question, and one he wanted to pursue.

'I was thinking of hiring a car and driving to the top of Mount Panorama. But it seemed a waste for just myself. All that lovely scenery, I mean,' he added casually, as if they hadn't just met, but were old friends.

His eyes fell casually to the diary which was held open on her lap. The writing looked a little faded, but it was definitely written by a female hand. Could it have been written by Angela Canfield-Hope herself?

He felt his hands clenching into fists, and quickly unclenched them again, lest she should see.

Persis closed the diary with a snap. 'Isn't it the home of a racing circuit now?' she asked. She vaguely remembered reading about it.

Dane nodded. 'The Bathurst 1000. I've always had a dream to come here one day and ride around it.'

Smile, say something polite and walk away, Persis thought. 'Then you must do it,' she heard herself saying coolly.

Dane Culver looked at her. 'Will you come with me?' he asked quietly.

Persis dragged in a deep breath. No. Absolutely not.

'Of course. I'd love to,' she said.

* * *

An hour later, she was sure she was going to die. He was driving fast, so very fast. But she realized, almost before her fear had time to begin, he also drove well. Very well indeed. And the fear simply went.

Now there was only speed and bright sunlight, and unfamiliar trees full of unfamiliar birds flashing past her window in a blur. And a sense of height, and of a land stretching off to infinity all around her. She didn't realize it, but she began to smile. And, in that smile, began to live again. Like a flower, blooming after a long, hard drought.

Dane, changing down the gears to take a bend, glanced across at her, and felt his heart leap. She looked so different when she was smiling.

He himself was enjoying the hair-raising ride immensely, but only, he realized in that moment, because of this woman beside him. Alone, the experience would have been so much flatter.

And although he knew it was folly, sheer, pure, bloody-minded stupidity, given that she was the enemy, he knew that he would do anything to make her smile again.

CHAPTER THREE

The Indian Pacific *and Broken Hill*

When Persis boarded the train that evening she was not at all surprised to see, a few carriages further down, the tall dark figure of Dane Culver also boarding. Not that he'd told her that he would be on the train, but she'd just known that, after their hair-raising ride on the race circuit together, things simply couldn't end there. There was a growing inevitability about her association with 'The Predator' which she was beginning to take almost for granted.

After their drive he'd taken her back to the park, asking her if she'd like to dine with him, but she'd declined, knowing she had a train to catch at 7.38 p.m., which would leave her little time. He'd seemed unsurprised by her refusal, and after a brief thanks for her company, and apologizing if he'd scared her, he'd simply walked away with an easy lope which ate up the ground and quickly took him from sight.

But not from mind.

Dane Culver. Just who was he? Now, watching him board the same train as herself, Persis wondered again. Their meeting in Sydney had to be accidental, didn't it? Just one of those things. But now they'd met again in Bathurst, so he too must be taking the train west. But he was an Australian and presumably lived in Sydney. Or did he? Perhaps he'd just been visiting too. He might live as far away as Perth. But if so, why didn't he just fly home? Could he have a fear of flying? Some people had a phobia so strong they went everywhere by rail, car or sea.

But then she remembered the ease with which he drove, changing gears, hugging the racing circuit, climbing the mountain higher and higher, faster and faster, and he'd never faltered. No, she was sure that Dane Culver and fear, fear of any kind, were virtual strangers to each other.

Could he simply be on holiday too? Most Australians, because of the vastness of their country, tended to live in one small part of it, and whenever they ventured into another area did so by plane, thus missing out on so much. Surely it wasn't only Europeans and other foreigners who yearned to see something of the outback a little more intimately than from 50,000 feet?

She boarded slowly, thoughtfully, in a mixture of trepidation and delight. No doubt about it, Dane Culver's company was intoxicating. But was she ready for it?

* * *

Rayne converted her chair into a single bed and brushed her teeth. She was getting used to the lulling motion of the train by now, and after a good dinner of pumpkin and crab meat salad, was feeling pleasantly sleepy.

Avery McLeod had proved to be a surprisingly witty and knowledgeable dinner companion. Most men, she'd found, after having successfully 'hooked' their fish, then proceeded to reel them in with an exaggerated story of their life or with a too-obvious attempt to 'listen' to her own. Avery McLeod, however, had been able to talk about anything from the latest bestselling novel to astrology, to serious classical music versus modern classical for the pop era, and all topics in between. She had enjoyed leading him down ever more complicated conversational paths, just to see if he could keep up. And he could. Pretty impressive, she knew, for a lad who'd had only a rudimentary education at a rather demoralized inner-city comprehensive. Even more impressive than that, though, had been the fact that when she had finally succeeded in stumping him, he'd simply laughed and owned up to it. Not many men, in her experience, could do that.

Now, as she put on the top half of a pair of men's pyjamas, which hung to just below her knees, she climbed into bed wearing a big smile.

What a guy. But still a crook.

The next morning, Rayne got up early and plugged in her laptop. Luckily, all her gear was compatible with the Australian electrical system, and as she drank orange juice she booted up and checked her email. As she clicked on to it, in the cabin next door, a small machine began beeping.

Felix Barstow stopped shaving and immediately went to his own laptop, which had a strange and extremely illegal little gadget attached to it. He was a slender man nearing his forties, with brown thinning hair and a small sharp face. His brown eyes narrowed as he quickly tapped buttons, eyes squinting down at the screen.

In her compartment, Rayne opened her email, unaware that she was also displaying it to the man next door on his screen. She quickly scanned it. It was from the insurance company's head office in Canary Wharf. With something like a ten-hour time difference, she knew it must be getting fairly late back home. Nice to see that Guy Varney, her PA, was on the ball and eager for promotion. Or overtime pay.

Just got fire marshal's official report. Definitely arson at Littledore Manor. Require set of suspect's prints. By sheer fluke, they tell me, a pane of glass not shattered is believed to be point of illegal entry, and a partial thumbprint has been found. Don't the bad guys believe in wearing gloves anymore? Send soonest. Guy.

Rayne pursed her lips thoughtfully.

Felix Barstow read it even more thoughtfully. Damn. How had that idiot Baines managed to leave a print behind? He was supposed to be the best damned arsonist going. The email said it was a fluke the glass wasn't shattered, but even so. Greg Nones wasn't going to like this. Not one little bit. Still, apart from that, things were progressing nicely.

Satisfied, he switched off the laptop, leaving the illegal little gizmo firmly in place, and calmly resumed shaving.

In her cabin, Rayne closed her laptop and went to breakfast early. They were due in Broken Hill at 8.50 a.m. so she would be hard pressed to get a set of Avery's fingerprints right now. She'd just have to wait until lunch.

When she went into the restaurant, it was nearly full. No doubt those travelling on after Broken Hill were waiting until the second sitting out of politeness, but there were still more than enough people leaving at the next stop to keep the stewards busy. She was a little disappointed not to see Avery. Lazy sod was probably still hugging the blankets. Then she felt a momentarily flutter of panic. What if he overslept? Missed the station? She'd have to stay on board too — and how would she explain that? Two people oversleeping on the same day was stretching it a bit far.

Damn.

She made her way to a table where a woman was sitting on her own. 'Excuse me, would you mind if I joined you? Or are you waiting for someone?'

The woman looked up, displaying big grey eyes set in a pale face which looked a little too thin. But she was a beauty for all that, Rayne thought, without jealousy. The dark mysterious type held no horrors for someone of her ilk.

Persis looked up and smiled at the sunny blonde. 'No, please. Do join me. You're a fellow Brit, aren't you?'

Rayne laughed and bounced into her seat, reaching for the menu. 'That's right. You're not waiting for a husband or anything, are you?'

Persis smiled. 'No,' she said softly. 'No husband.' If things had worked out with Rob though . . . But they hadn't. And, in fact, it wasn't Rob's face which immediately popped into her mind but the dark, rather sardonic features of Dane Culver.

Dane, who was sitting just three tables down. She'd noticed him the moment she'd come into the room. Was he getting off at Broken Hill? What would she do if he was? If he asked her out again? She knew she wanted him to, even though her head and her heart were in direct opposition to each other, one urging her to have nothing to do with him, the other egging her on.

But what if he *didn't* get off at Broken Hill? What if she never saw him again? Her rather Mona Lisa-like smile flitted away and Rayne found herself doing a double take. Her table companion looked rather sad, she thought. Something about her made Rayne feel a little heartsore. She shook her head briskly and buried her nose in the menu. Other people's woes were nothing to do with her. She had enough on her own plate. Nevertheless, she couldn't just sit there and let the other woman suffer in silence.

'The fruit salad looks good,' she said thoughtfully. It was, according to the menu, comprised of orange, rockmelon, honeydew, grapes, pineapple and passion fruit.

'It is,' Persis agreed. 'But you should try the special coffee as well. They make it with wattle seeds, native around desert areas. It gives coffee a nice, nutty kind of flavour.'

'That'll do me then.' Rayne, always up to trying something new, nodded happily. 'Getting off at the next stop, are you?'

Persis nodded vaguely. And as she did so, she noticed Dane Culver glance at his watch then get up. Her heart did a little jig. That must mean he was checking up on the time, and leaving to get his things together. Surely he'd be getting off at the next stop too? It worried her a little at how desperately she needed to be right.

'Excuse me, I must go,' Persis murmured, and Rayne watched her leave, a speculative look in her eyes. Now either she was no judge of character, or that lady had things on her mind. She shrugged, then smiled at the steward who approached, making the poor man almost lose his footing. Looking down into big blue eyes which seemed to smoke him right down to his toenails, he gulped.

'Tea or coffee, madam?' he asked, in his broad Australian accent.

'Oh, coffee, please,' Rayne said, enjoying the man's lightly shaking hand as he poured out her cup. It was nice to be young and attractive and many miles from home. It gave a girl a wonderful sense of freedom.

Just then the carriage door opened and Avery walked in. His hair was damp from a shower and looking a little darker than usual, and he was dressed in a short-sleeved T-shirt of the palest coffee colour and dark brown slacks. He looked like a chocolate bar, waiting to be eaten.

And Rayne loved chocolate.

She smiled and waved a hand in greeting to attract his attention. The steward sighed and moved on to the next table.

* * *

In her cabin, Persis made sure everything was packed then sat in her chair, glancing outside. The earth was so vivid, an orange-red colour, that it looked unreal. Small green bushes pockmarked the vast expanse of land and away to her right, stretching off into infinity, was a barbed-wire fence, the posts running in a perfectly straight line for miles and miles, as far as her eye could see. What a strange land, and utterly alien to a girl who was used to the green and pleasant meadows of rural England.

No wonder her grandmother had described it as like being on another planet. Long before the age of space travel or even much science-fiction literature, Angela Canfield-Hope had likened this very same landscape to what she imagined to be the playing fields of Mars.

She sighed with regret as the town of Broken Hill began to appear, and soon the train was pulling into the station. With a deep breath, she gathered up her things and alighted. The dry hot air hit her like a physical force as she stepped from the air-conditioned train. She refused to look around at her fellow passengers, however. If Dane Culver was not, after all, getting off here, she didn't want to know it.

It scared her, the thought that he had so much power to hurt her. But then, she was beginning to suspect that the tall, dark, quiet Australian had far more power over her than the mere ability to cause her pain.

She stepped from the railway station onto Crystal Street, and walked slowly to a bench set in the shade. With her bags beside her, she watched taxis come and go, as departing passengers gobbled them up and sped away.

Removing a brochure from her bag, she opened it, and was struck at once by a photograph. Taken at sunset, it showed a rock which looked like (and in fact was) a carved piece of art, standing in the desert. The Living Desert Sculptures, she read, were one of the city's most spectacular tourist attractions and could be reached by heading up the hill, approximately a twenty-minute walk away. A small price to pay in order to admire the work of the artists who'd sculpted such wonders out of centuries-old rock.

She would definitely have to do that. But later. Right now . . .

'Would you like a lift?'

Slowly Persis glanced up. 'Yes, please,' she said softly.

Dane nodded. 'I've got a taxi waiting. Do you know where you're staying?'

Persis shook her head. 'No. I usually pick a hotel from the brochure and hope for the best.'

Dane nodded, a shade grimly. It was hardly a sensible plan and he wanted, suddenly, to shake her and ask her just what the hell she thought she was doing, wandering around at the far end of the world when she hardly looked as if she could take care of herself in her own back garden. What if a festival had been on? What if every room in every joint from the best hotel to the lowest cut-rate boarding house had been taken? What would she do then? Sleep on a park bench?

For a second, Persis wondered if something was wrong. His jaw clenched and his eyes flashed like the warning illumination of lightning in a far-off thundercloud. Then he smiled.

'I've got a room booked at the Lodge Motel. Shall we see if they have a spare?' He had pre-booked a room at a good hotel in towns throughout the train route. He was a man who liked to be prepared, although he'd never been in the boy scouts.

Persis smiled. 'It sounds nice. Thank you.' She got up and reached for a bag, then hastily let it go again as the muscles in her arms, slightly atrophied through her long bout of illness, refused to co-operate.

Dane quickly retrieved it. 'Here, let me,' he said. It didn't seem that heavy. Unlike most women when travelling, she had been pretty restrained. No kitchen sink, at any rate.

He glanced at her and she flushed, imagining a question where there was none. 'I've not been all that well recently,' she felt compelled to explain, missing the way his face went utterly still.

'Oh?'

Persis reached for the lighter of the two bags, firmly hoisting it over one shoulder. 'But I'm all right now.'

Dane smiled, but it was mechanical. Already he was recalling the way she'd stumbled at the café back in Sydney. And now that he thought about it, what had she stumbled over? There'd been no step.

'I noticed that you look pale,' he said conversationally, as they headed for the taxi patiently waiting, 'but I put it down to the usual pom's pallor.'

Persis laughed. 'Hospital pallor in my case,' she said, and thought she heard him draw his breath in harshly. But when she quickly turned her head, he was looking blandly down at the taxi driver. 'The Lodge, please, mate,' he said, and opened the back door for her.

Inside, he carefully placed her packed holdall between his feet. 'Nothing serious, I hope?' he asked, trying to sound casual.

Persis smiled but simply shook her head. She was not about to go into the rather humiliating experience which was an undiagnosed, vague disease. She knew some of her so-called friends had even wondered aloud, and behind her back, if she'd been ill at all. In the physical sense of the word, that is. Or if Rob leaving her had sent her into some kind of mental decline.

No. She definitely wasn't about to go into *that* with Dane Culver. So she looked out of the window and watched the town go by, not realizing that she'd left him with a cold sense of dread.

Dane glanced across at her and noted the very fine and prominent bone structure of her face. Was she dying? Was that why she'd come to Australia? His hands, once clenched into fists of rage, now sweated helplessly.

* * *

The Lodge did indeed have room for Persis, and as soon as she'd left him in the lobby, Dane was on the phone. The PI company he'd used before was in his phone memory, and he quickly dialled it while walking to his own room, not even bothering to wait for privacy. When he got through, he told them what he wanted. And fast.

Afterwards, he paced his room for a while, shaking his head. She couldn't be dying. She just couldn't. It wasn't *fair*. He'd only just found her . . . He brought his thoughts to a halt right there, right then.

What the hell was he *thinking*?

* * *

'What do you think? Casuarina Cottage or Rose Cottage?' Avery asked.

After their hurried breakfast together, they'd just had time to check out the accommodation available in the Broken Hill brochures before the train pulled into the station, and Rayne had spotted the 'historic cottages' advertised. Pointing out that this was just the sort of deluxe accommodation that his customers could expect, Avery had quickly agreed to check them out. Luckily, they'd gone straight there, for there were only two left to choose from.

Now Rayne cocked her bright head a little to one side, and made a moue with her mouth. Instantly, Avery's eyes went to the rose-coloured lips and he smiled.

'We'll take Rose Cottage,' he said to the desk clerk.

'Hey!' Rayne said in protest.

'If we have to wait for a woman to make up her mind we'll be here all day, right?' Avery said to the clerk, deliberately living dangerously.

'S'right, mate,' the desk clerk said, playing along.

Rayne narrowed her eyes, catlike, at Avery, silently promising all kinds of retribution later, and Avery felt his heartbeat quicken. He was, in truth, more than willing to pay later, and was finding it rather hard to believe his luck. Who'd have thought, so far from home, that he'd find a little gem like Rayne? She seemed to be everything he was looking for in a girl — adventurous, fun-loving, intelligent, beautiful.

She had to be married, or at least spoken for, back home. He was probably her one last wild fling before settling down. Normally, he'd have been only too pleased to step forward for the role. A no-strings love affair far from your own back doorstep was most men's favourite fantasy, wasn't it? So why did the thought of all this coming to an end just over a week from now, when they finally hit Perth, make him feel so flat?

Taking a deep breath as he followed her to Rose Cottage, a pretty little single-storey building with — of course — roses in front of it, he told himself to be careful.

Very careful. Something told him he was handling dynamite.

* * *

There were two bedrooms which, Rayne told him firmly, was just as well, otherwise it would have been the couch for him. Not knowing if she was joking or not, Avery shrugged and held up his hands in the universal peace sign.

'So, where first?' he asked, sounding all businesslike, but with his eyes firmly fixed on the V-shaped section of pink-and-white skin between her breasts. She'd changed into a pale pink top, one of those which tie in a knot at the waist, and with very short shorts in a hot-pink shade to accompany it, it was a toss-up whether he tried to keep his eyes from her legs or her more rounded curves. Happily, he was failing in both departments.

Rayne grinned. 'Down, boy,' she said, aware of his dark, somnolent and wickedly wandering eyes. 'The galleries, I think, don't you?'

Avery groaned.

'Come on,' she said. 'Think of your Cloud Nine customers, all hot and eager to savour some culture.'

Muttering something dire about just what he'd like to do with culture, Avery followed her out of the door, his eyes fixed, as she'd intended, on her luscious derrière.

Three hours (and the Broken Hill City Art Gallery, the Pro Hart Gallery and the Historical Photo Gallery) later, they called a halt and headed for the nearby Caledonian Hotel, near a church just off Oxide and Chloride Streets.

It was late, the majority of the lunchtime crowd having already been and gone, so Rayne ordered a quick and easy Caesar salad, and Avery a lamb chop.

'Let's treat ourselves to an Australian wine,' Rayne said, thinking of the nice clear prints a glass took.

Avery obligingly ran his eye over the wine list and opted for something Rayne had never heard of before, and when it came, along with the food, it turned out to be a crisp, tangy white wine which left a lovely vanilla aftertaste on her palate.

'So, what do you do for a living?' Avery asked, spearing a new potato and almost making Rayne choke on her wine.

'Oh, nothing very glamorous,' she said quickly. She already had a whole false life mapped out, of course, right down to phoney schools and phoney job. 'I'm a secretary at a small law firm. They do mostly house sales, that sort of thing. Nothing juicy. Nothing criminal.'

She watched him carefully as she said the last sentence, but he was cutting into his meat and didn't even flicker so much as an eyelid. But then, she wouldn't have expected him to give himself away.

Not this man. She was getting to know him now. He was the kind who was competent at anything he set out to do. Confident without being cocky. Clever without being smug. The sort who probably *would* get away with a million-pound insurance fraud. *If* the insurance investigator had been anyone other than Rayne Eloise Fletcher, that is.

'I spend my life typing letters to recalcitrant landlords, fibbing estate agents and desperate homeowners. Now you can see why I craved some adventure on this holiday,' she carried on. And wondered what he'd do if she told him that, as a girl, it had been her ambition to join the police force. So much so that she'd actually joined up, gone through all the training and even spent a year walking the beat before she realized that the male hierarchy was simply too entrenched; that it would be years before she'd get to do the kind of jobs she wanted to do, had she remained.

No doubt that would have made him sit up and take notice. And if she'd told him that right after leaving the police she'd been taken on and trained by one of Reut's top investigators to become an insurance investigator herself, not even the supercool Mr Avery McLeod would be able to sit so calmly eating his meal.

Or would he?

A pang of sexual tension, hot and deep between her legs, made her wonder if, in this man, she might have met her match at last.

During the past four years she'd been successful in catching out all sorts of con artists. From the corporate kind, who hid behind lackeys and lawyers, to the pathetic single owner in over his head. She'd seen the fall of yuppie big-city whizz-kids, and seasoned, grizzled veterans. None, however, she was beginning to realize, were in this man's class.

So she'd definitely have to be careful. No letting things slip.

She waited until he excused himself after the meal and then carefully slipped her serviette around his glass, emptying the contents into her own. After taking a careful look around, she slipped his original glass into her bag, drank the wine in her glass down to the level she had poured in, then put it at his place setting. She'd leave an extra-large tip to cover its theft and salve her conscience.

Then, sometime in the afternoon, she'd have to make some excuse to slip away and post it off special delivery to London. After taking a set of prints for her own use, of course. She could do that. It had given her a great thrill, as a raw police recruit, to play with powder and brushes and tape, and take her very first set of 'dabs'.

Now, of course, it had become strictly routine.

* * *

Felix Barstow watched Rayne Fletcher and Avery McLeod leave their accommodation and walk hand in hand across the road. When they reached the other side, his lips twisted sardonically as the blonde insurance investigator reached up on tiptoe and kissed her mark. He saw the way Avery's arms tightened around her and saw the blonde's curvaceous, petite figure melt against his.

And his cynical smile slowly turned into a scowl.

That looked pretty much like the real thing to him. Or was the ditzy blonde just a very good actress? Damn. If the stupid cow really was falling for him, it could screw up the whole plan. Felix knew from bitter experience that you couldn't trust a woman, especially one who thought herself in love. They were apt to do the craziest of things.

As he watched them walk away, arm in arm, his busy little ferret-like brain began to scheme.

Backup plans were something Felix Barstow always liked to have handy. After his first stint in jail he'd learned the need for them, and they had kept him out of trouble for many years since.

Yes, it was definitely time to consider a plan B.

* * *

Persis dined that night at the motel with Dane. They both chose fish and ordered a second bottle of one of Australia's justly famous wines, and later, on the dance floor, she found herself in his arms.

The floor was lit with small diamond shapes from an overhead globe, and the band, a local bluegrass outfit, played a slightly mournful tune. It felt good, resting her head against his shoulder, feeling his arm around her waist, his hand splayed against her back. She was wearing a plain white evening dress with a deep V at the back, and his thumb and one finger rested on her bare skin, warming it, making tiny radiations of heat span out, leaving her feeling pleasantly flushed.

Afterwards, he walked her to her room. At the door, she paused awkwardly, then looked up at him. In the dim light of the passageway, his eyes were dark and mysterious, one half of his face in shadow, giving him a deliciously sinister look.

Her heart raced. 'It's been lovely,' she said simply. But meant it. Shyly, almost in a show of manners, her face tilted up for his kiss and Dane felt his whole body contract.

Well, he'd asked for it. Dinner and dancing. Now, not surprisingly, the lady expected a kiss. And he would have given anything not to oblige her. Because, before his lips had even touched hers, he knew what it would do to him.

Persis felt first his hand on her hip, then his face lowering to hers, blotting out the light; her eyes feathered closed. His lips touched hers, light, cool, yet with an underlying heat which seemed to touch her on the tips of her breasts, the tops of her thighs, and some place not physical, but centred deep in her psyche.

She took a surprised gasp, drawing the air from his very lungs, this ultimate in intimate actions making his hand tighten on her, and his kiss deepen. When he dragged his head up, she nearly fell forward, so far was she leaning against him, relying on his strength.

Bewildered, highly happy but deeply uneasy at the same time, she opened her eyes and found his own glittering down at her, a look almost of hatred on his face.

It made something hot and savage and previously unknown to her leap from deep within; and for a moment, a wild, insane, utterly mad moment, she wanted to reach out, to dig her fingernails into the side of his face, and drag his head back to hers so that she could kiss that look right out of his eyes.

Then it passed, leaving her shaken and feeling curiously naked. Vulnerable.

What on earth was this man doing to her?

'Goodnight, Dane,' she gulped, and fled into her room.

Dane watched the door slam in his face and cursed. Deep and low. And with feeling.

CHAPTER FOUR

The Indian Pacific *and Adelaide*

Dane pulled the door of the restaurant car open and stepped back to let Persis go ahead. The train had left Broken Hill at nine o'clock, just a few minutes ago, and they'd decided to wait and breakfast on the train. As they'd hoped, the car was virtually deserted, and as they took their seats Dane glanced out at a passing town and sighed. 'It's sad to leave Broken Hill so soon,' he muttered. 'Charles Rasp was always a hero of mine.'

'Charles Rasp?' she repeated questioningly, trying to forget all about The Kiss last night. Not easy, since she'd tossed and turned all night remembering it in vivid detail, until it had taken on a significance way out of proportion with the event. Now she was glad to grasp onto any conversational gambit in the hopes of acting like a rational, civilized human being.

'Yes. He was a boundary rider back in 1883. Something about the rocks told him it would be a good place to dig, and it was. And not your typical flash-in-the-pan goldmine, here today and gone tomorrow, either. There were massive deposits of lead, zinc and silver. Later they discovered uranium.

Even now, the town produces two million tonnes of it every year.'

Persis nodded. So that was why the streets were named so oddly! 'You sound very knowledgeable. Are you in the mining industry?'

Dane's hand tightened on the coffee cup he was holding. They'd both ordered cereal, neither of them being much in the mood for food, and now, with a single question, she'd left him reeling. Should he lie? The sensible thing would be to do just that, but he was getting heartily sick of this whole charade. He wanted it out in the open where he could tackle it head-on.

'That's right. I'm the chairman of Culver Mines,' he said, and waited.

But nothing happened. Persis simply nodded. She realized by the way he'd said it that he expected a reaction, but she was not Australian, and had never heard of it. Was he famous? Was he expecting her to know about him? Or was he just making conversation? 'That sounds interesting,' she said carefully, leaving her options open, and Dane blinked. He couldn't believe it. There had been no reaction at all. What was this? Was she an ace poker player, used to keeping a blank face in spite of any amount of pressure? Or did she actually not know? Could that be possible?

'So do you mine gold?' she asked, sounding genuinely interested, he noted. But only in the way which anyone might be interested in a lifestyle so different from their own. And not at all like someone with a vested interest. Slowly, Dane let out a long, harsh breath. He hadn't realized until now just how uptight he'd been.

'No,' he said slowly. 'Opals.' And tensed right up again. Surely now the penny would drop, and he'd see dismay, perhaps even fear, cloud those lovely grey eyes of hers.

But Persis smiled in delight. 'Opals! How lovely. I've always thought they were such wonderful things. Sort of mysterious. Not like other precious stones at all.'

Dane just managed to stop himself from sneering. So she thought opals were wonderful, did she? She had to be her grandmother's progeny after all. But why was she still playing Little Miss Innocent?

'I mine other things too,' he said. 'But opals are my first love. They mean a lot to the family.'

Persis didn't mistake the gravitas in his voice. And from the way he was looking at her, so closely, she sensed that she was supposed to infer something from it. But what? She still knew so little about him.

'I can imagine,' she said gently. 'I run a gallery with a friend of mine, and I know how I feel when I come across a genuine find. It actually makes my toes tingle. But that's not the same as literally digging treasures out of the ground. Tell me about them. Opals, I mean.'

It seemed to Persis a perfectly safe thing to ask. He'd told her he was a miner and that he loved opals. So why was he looking at her like that? Why was he staring at her as if trying to read her soul? Or was she just imagining it? Perhaps he was remembering their kiss last night, and was trying to figure out what had happened, as she'd done.

She wondered if she was blushing, and hoped not.

Dane, after a long thoughtful pause, took a deep breath. One of them was playing with fire with this conversation, and he was not at all convinced that it was Persis Canfield-Hope.

'Well, let's see,' he said. 'Opals are a natural form of amorphous, non-crystalline silica. Or Si02, as we geologists call it.'

'You have a degree in geology?' she put in quickly, but was somehow not surprised. The man's brain power was beginning to shine through as clearly as his sexual charisma.

Dane nodded. 'From Adelaide Uni, in fact.'

'Tell me more about opals. Aren't they rather special in some way? I mean different from emeralds or diamonds or what have you?' she pressed, wanting, woman-like, to know every last thing about him. And especially the things which were important to him.

Dane smiled dryly. 'Yes, they are different,' he drawled. As if she, and the rest of the Canfield-Hopes didn't know.

But would she really have the nerve to go on like this if she knew about the past? He was beginning to hope not. He was *very much* beginning to hope not. This grim little reminder of the way his wayward heart was heading forced him to concentrate on the task at hand. So he watched her like a hawk as he continued on, but not once did he catch any glimpse of duplicity or fear in her eyes.

'It's because they contain water, so you have to keep them out of dry conditions whenever possible, or they can crack. They're usually white, but have a characteristic play of *rainbow* colours in them.'

Was it her imagination, or did he stress the word 'rainbow' just then? She wasn't sure why, but in that moment she had the feeling that something else was going on. Something that had nothing to do with the 'getting-to-know-you' stage of potential lovers.

She felt her insides melt a little at the thought, but she was not about to dodge the issue. They were potential lovers, weren't they? If they weren't, then what on earth had last night's kiss been all about?

Persis was well aware that she was more or less new at this sort of thing. The only other man she'd ever slept with was Rob, and that, she was beginning to think, may not have been as successful or as fulfilling as it might have been. Because just one kiss from this man had made her feel more throughout her entire body than a night spent in Rob's bed.

Surely that knowledge would frighten any woman?

But even so, some other kind of warning system was ringing in her head. Was he married, perhaps? Could that be it? But his ring fingers were clear. Into her head popped the thought of her grandmother, coming all this way only to fall in love with a married man. Was she scared she was making the same mistake?

'Are you married?' she asked bluntly, then flushed. Subtle or what? But she really needed to know.

Dane blinked. 'No. Divorced. Four years ago, no children. And you?' But he already knew the answer. His PI firm had done a basic family background check on all the Canfield-Hopes.

'No. I was almost engaged once. Or thought I was,' she said, somewhat confusingly. 'But he was nothing,' she added, saddened and surprised by how true that suddenly was.

Dane just stopped himself from reaching out and touching her hand, sensing her need for comfort. Damn it, he was going to have to be careful. This woman was going to tie him in knots if he didn't watch out. And they both knew what the results of that could be. But whereas Dane had his grandfather's example as a warning about Canfield-Hope women, he still wasn't convinced that Persis herself had any idea of their family's shared history. It was imperative that he find out, for his own peace of mind, if nothing else. And because of what was happening in Perth.

That reminded him. He would have to call her soon.

Persis looked out at the passing world beyond the train's window, recalling a mental map of the route and knowing that at some point during this journey they'd start dipping south, towards Adelaide. Outside, a huge flock of white cockatoos lifted off, and she caught her breath, lost in the enchantment of the scene.

'It's the cattle troughs,' Dane said, enjoying the look of simple wonder and childlike pleasure on her face. 'The troughs are always full, attracting the birds.'

The rolling sea of red sand dunes, topped by stunted mallee trees and low desert grasses, seemed to go on for ever. She knew that, in the Menindee, kangaroos and emus gathered to feed. But she could see none now.

'No wonder my grandmother fell in love with this place,' she said, missing the way Dane suddenly stiffened to attention.

He opened his mouth to question her, then abruptly closed it again. If she was playing games with him, he had to let her. He could learn a lot that way. And if she wasn't playing games . . . well, he could still learn a lot.

He experienced a moment of unease, his conscience pricking him with a harshness that he didn't like. But then

Persis was talking again, and the moment when he might have spoken was suddenly gone.

'She came here between the wars,' Persis carried on, smiling at him. 'My mother found her diary when I was in hospital and brought it in for me to read. She thought it would cheer me up. I never knew her, you see. She died before I was born.'

Dane leaned back impatiently as the steward cleared the table. 'But I dare say your family spoke of her often,' he said, somewhat harshly. They must have. The triumphant Angela. How could they not boast about her?

'No, not really,' Persis said, unaware that she had so much of his undivided and puzzled attention. 'But when I started to read her diary, I wished they had. She was something of a free spirit, I think. In the thirties, not many women would have travelled to Australia alone, to roam from coast to coast, seeing life and tasting freedom,' she said. 'I suppose she was very brave. That's how come she died, during the Blitz. It was nearly at the very end of the war, but instead of staying in the bomb shelter with my mother, who was just a few weeks old at the time, she went out and helped to rescue others from a burning building. A neighbour, I think. She managed to get out the children but died when the roof collapsed. I think she must have been some woman.'

Dane blinked. Although he couldn't help admiring bravery, he was incapable of saying anything which lauded Angela Canfield-Hope. He knew that she'd married a few years after returning home, of course, from the PI reports, and also that she had divorced her husband after only a year and reverted back to her maiden name. The child of the marriage, Persis's mother, had also, unusually, retained the Canfield-Hope name.

'From her diary, I learned a lot about this country back then,' Persis continued. 'So when the doctors told me to take a few months to recuperate, I thought, why not come over here and follow in her footsteps? Who knows, I might even find Iris.'

Dane spilled his coffee. Not surprising, since his hand jerked so hard.

'Iris?' he managed to croak.

Persis reached for a napkin, and helped him to mop up the spillage. 'Yes. I think I might have a long-lost aunt over here. Her diary is a bit mysterious on the point. She had a lover, I think, probably a married man. And I think she *might* have had a love child with him. She refers to her "beautiful Iris" several times in her diary. And about how much her lover meant to her. Somewhere she talks about how he gave her the most precious thing she had — Iris. Don't you think that's romantic?'

Dane was incapable of speech.

'Except she must have been forced to leave her daughter behind,' Persis continued with a sigh. 'Oh, not because she was ashamed to have an illegitimate child; I can't see my grandmother caring about that! But maybe because of the rumours of war that were going around by then. I'm sure she would have felt that her daughter would be safer here in Australia. I know for a fact that her diary talks about the day she'd come back, so she always intended to return for her, I'm sure. Perhaps that's why her marriage was over so quickly. I often wonder if her lover over here ever knew what had happened to her,' she finished wistfully. Dane looked away as she turned her big grey eyes towards him. 'What do you think?'

'I don't know,' he said. But he did. His grandfather had never known why his beloved Angela had never returned. The family had always assumed she'd found someone else to sink her claws into. Someone rich, of course. Although Persis's grandfather had not been all that wealthy. Perhaps that's why she'd been so quick to divorce him — he hadn't come up to standard.

'Well, we'd best go,' she said, glancing around guiltily, realizing they were the last ones left in the restaurant.

Dane nodded vaguely, but his head was reeling. He had a lot to think about.

* * *

In her cabin, Rayne read her email while, once again, in his own cabin next door, Felix Barstow did the same.

> *Fingerprints received, and don't match the partial at Littledore. I guess it was too much to hope for. Guy.*

Rayne let out a long, slow breath and leaned back in her chair, switching off the machine. She knew she shouldn't be feeling so relieved, but she was. Damn it, she knew better than this. Just because Avery McLeod hadn't set fire to that worthless sinkhole which was Littledore Manor didn't mean he hadn't hired somebody else to do his dirty work for him.

She was surprised, though. In her experience, crooks came in two varieties. The kind who paid others to do the dirty work for them and those who, not liking to be at the mercy of someone else, did it themselves. And she had firmly put Avery into the latter class. She was sure it wasn't beyond him to read up on the subject and do a first-class piece of arson on a property.

In fact, the more she thought about it, the less she liked it. They knew Avery had purchased the run-down, structurally dodgy eighteenth-century Littledore Manor in Gloucestershire just four months ago. They had his signature on all the documents to prove it. They knew he was (or rather, *said* he was) going to upgrade the manor and turn it into a first-class hotel. Set in the Cotswolds, it was, according to Cloud Nine's joint chairman, the perfect building to begin the company's sojourn into the hotel-owning business. Except that it would have taken more money than Cloud Nine had to refurbish it properly, even if subsidence hadn't been a problem.

So the place had mysteriously burned down, which would have given Cloud Nine a very nice little insurance payout. If Reut, Cole and Phipps hadn't smelled a rat, and sent Rayne to investigate, that is. For though the arson had been good, it had not been quite good enough.

What's more, only Avery McLeod's signature showed on the insurance documentation, Greg Nones, the other partner, being left out in the cold apparently.

It just didn't smell right, Rayne thought now. It didn't feel right, either. Would someone as on the ball as Avery really not realize what a clunker he was buying in Littledore? And then to hire someone to torch it, while very obviously leaving his partner out of the whole scheme, was just so . . . clumsy. So obvious.

Rayne leapt to her feet as there was a knock at the door. A second later, Avery opened it and looked in, immediately filling the small space with the scent, sight and sound of him. She could hear him breathing, and the crisp, cool scent of his cologne tingled her nose. 'Hello, here you are. Hiding from me, are you?' he teased.

'Nope,' Rayne said. 'I was just wondering when you'd get here.'

He grinned and walked in. 'Thinking about me?' he asked huskily, reaching for her.

'You have no idea,' she murmured as she stood up on tiptoe to kiss him.

* * *

Adelaide was just lighting up when Rayne and Avery left their hotel to explore, heading for Hindley Street and the North Terrace, the city's main entertainment precinct.

'Let's hit the casino,' Avery suggested, linking his arm through hers. She wore a short white dress and chunky gold jewellery, and looked glamorous enough for a palace.

'I didn't know you were a gambler,' she said, wondering if that explained things.

'I'm not. I leave that to Greg,' he said shortly, something in his tone making her look at him quickly. 'But you look gorgeous, and I want to show you off,' he added with a wolfish smile. 'I like walking into a room and having every man in the place look daggers at me, just because I have the most beautiful girl in the world on my arm.'

'Flattery will get you somewhere,' she said mysteriously, but wasn't willing to let it go. 'You sound as if you don't like your partner. Does he have a serious problem, or were you joking?'

Avery sighed. 'Yes and no. Greg *does* have a problem, but then it's his money, not mine. He has independent means, as the saying goes,' he explained as they entered the casino. Rayne watched him cash in some money for a modest amount of chips. 'It's the only reason I went in with him in the first place. I'd never have been able to start up Cloud Nine without his capital. But I do all the real work, the running of the show.'

'You still sound as if you don't like him much,' she pressed, sensing that it could be important.

Avery shrugged, not wanting to go into it. 'I'm thinking of splitting up the partnership, anyway. Now Cloud Nine's up and running, I might be able to buy him out.'

'Oh,' Rayne said, somewhat flatly. If he was unhappy and wanted to get rid of a partner who sounded like a real albatross around his neck, it might explain why he needed some capital to buy his way clear. And a big insurance payout would solve that problem nicely. Damn.

It wouldn't hurt her to get a copy of his handwriting, she mused, watching him place a bet at the baccarat table before moving on. Especially a copy of his signature. At some point, they'd need it to confirm that he'd instigated the policy if nothing else. Should the case ever get to court.

She knew why she was thinking such thoughts now, of course. Making herself think of work and the dictates of her job was also forcing herself to remember that he was a crook. For she had begun to hope that he wasn't, and that could be bad news indeed.

As she watched him place a bet on the roulette wheel, reacting without rancour or surprise as he lost, she found herself wishing that things were different. That she really was on holiday and lucky enough to have hooked up with a good-looking, loaded, fun-loving guy.

As Avery looked up at her and winked, his eyes caressive and full of promise, she forced herself to smile brightly back.

'What say we hit the pie carts after this,' she said, determined to be cheerful. 'From casinos to classic eateries. We have to check it all out, right?'

'Right,' he agreed, rather sotto voce.

She wondered how long she'd be able to hold him off. A man expected to get physical, after all. A girl too, for that matter! 'Oh, before I forget,' she added, deliberately darkly, 'I want your address and telephone number. Here,' she reached into her sparkling, beaded bag and withdrew a pen and paper. She watched, her hard heart aching just a little as he scribbled it out. Don't forget to sign your name,' she said, raising an eyebrow. 'After all, by the time I get home I expect to have a whole Filofax full of good-looking men's names and addresses from down under. I might forget which one you were.'

Avery grinned and obligingly signed his name to the scrap of paper. 'Sometimes I wonder when you're joking,' he said. And something in his eyes, something just a touch hurt, made her hard heart ache just that bit more. Was he trying to hint that he was beginning to feel something special for her?

Hell, she hoped not.

'Don't be daft,' she said, and reached up to kiss him. Hard. And once she'd done so, her body treacherously melted against him, needing more, wanting more. Determined to have more.

Damn.

Why did he have to be a crook?

* * *

The next morning, Felix Barstow found a public phone booth and dialled a UK number. 'Greg? It's me. How are things?' He listened for a while, then nodded. 'So you're almost set to do the flit? Make sure the bank doesn't get suspicious. No, not the cops — the Inland Revenue.' He paused, then listened some more. Then nodded. 'Don't worry. I'll plant the evidence within the next day or two.' Not, he thought with some irritation, that it would be all that easy. They were on and off that bloody train like yo-yos. He'd have to pick a time when they'd be spending a good long stretch on the tracks. At some point, the blonde was bound to search her mark's cabin. 'You just take things easy your end,' he said, and hung up.

He lit a cigarette, furiously thinking.

It might be a good idea if Avery McLeod didn't get back to the UK. If he was dead, he wouldn't be around to answer any questions at all, and then his role as the ideal scapegoat would be even more perfect.

He'd have to think about it.

* * *

Dane Culver had a quick breakfast, then rang Perth, waiting for the switchboard to put him through. His fingers tightened on the wire as the sound of her voice, pitifully weak and uneven, came over the wire. 'Yes?'

'Hello, sweetheart,' he said softly. 'It's me.'

'Do you have it yet?' she asked quickly, desperately.

'No, not yet. There might be a bit of a wrinkle.' And he told her about his talk with Persis yesterday.

'So she's dead. Angela, I mean,' the tired voice said wearily. 'How strange. I always knew that she must be by now, and I thought I would feel glad. But I don't.'

Dane nodded. 'I know. I'm finding everything rather weird too. And I'm beginning to think that Persis really doesn't know what happened.'

'Be careful,' the voice warned sharply, and Dane sighed.

'I know. I will be. Don't worry about me.' He wished, now, that he hadn't mentioned it. 'It's odd though. About Iris,' he said thoughtfully. 'Persis seemed genuinely convinced that Iris is a long-lost aunt.'

'Or maybe she only seems to be,' the voice warned him.

'Yes, perhaps,' Dane agreed flatly.

'Dane. I must get Iris back.' The voice, failing now, was hardly audible above the sound of telephone static.

'You will. Don't worry, you will,' Dane promised, and after a few more whispered endearments, hung up. He stood for a while, staring out of the window, then left to pick up Persis.

He would have to move things along much faster now. Even if she was as innocent as she seemed, he couldn't afford to be gentle with her.

* * *

Adelaide's Botanical Gardens and Bicentennial Conservatory was in North Terrace. Tranquil and spacious, they were begun in 1855 and Persis fell in love with them at first sight. As well as lawns, trees and rare subtropical and Mediterranean plant displays, the gardens had the oldest glasshouse in an Australian botanical garden. The nearby conservatory contained a complete tropical rainforest, and as they walked through it, Persis began to wilt in the heat and humidity, but was determined not to leave. 'It's breathtaking,' she said. And was indeed breathless.

'Yes. But you're looking all done in. Come on,' he said firmly, and walked her outside. Her knees, in truth, were beginning to buckle, and he steered her to the nearest restroom. 'Here, wash your face and wrists in cold water. It will help,' he said firmly.

It wasn't until she had gone inside that he realized she'd left her bag with him. He stared down at it by his feet, then squatted neatly onto his haunches and looked inside. And there it was. The diary.

Quickly, and without a moment's qualm now, he opened it and began to scan the pages. At first it was hard to read, for the writing was small and feminine. And, he quickly realized, a lot of it was in a personal kind of shorthand, with only the odd titillating word or sentence making sense.

Then his eyes found the words 'Walter C', and he knew that, at least in part, Persis hadn't lied to him. Slipping quickly through the pages, knowing that she might emerge at any moment, he realized that Angela Canfield-Hope had always referred to her mysterious married lover as Walter C. Never Walter Cartwright. So there was no reason for Persis to react to the name Culver — if she didn't know his grandfather's surname was Cartwright, she couldn't have traced the family line down to the Culvers. He felt his heart lift at this tentative proof in her favour.

But what of Iris?

He moved to the latter pages, but out of the corner of his eye saw the door begin to move and quickly thrust the diary back into the bag and straightened up.

'My, that's better. I was beginning to feel a bit faint,' Persis said, glancing slightly puzzled at her bag. What was he doing with it?

'It fell over, spilling things,' Dane said, all but thrusting it into her hands, feeling about two inches high. But, dammit, he had to get a copy of that damned diary. Even if it meant breaking into her hotel room one of these days and photographing it, page by page.

'Oh, thanks,' she said quietly.

'Come on, let's get you something to drink. And then we'll sit somewhere cool,' he said firmly.

Persis smiled. 'Sounds like heaven,' she agreed. She supposed, in this modern day and age, she should resent his taking charge like this. But in truth, it made her feel safe and cared for.

A few minutes later, an ice-cold fruit juice in her hand, she lay down on Dane's shirt between several beautiful flowering shrubs, deep in the shade of the garden's most quiet corner, and sighed blissfully. Birds rustled around them and, as she sipped, she tried to keep her eyes from Dane's bare back. He was sat beside her, watching a large bee drone in the head of an immense purple flower.

Persis wondered what he'd do if she reached out and ran her fingertip down the length of his spine. It had been gentlemanly of him to take off his shirt, to save her sitting on the bare grass and to protect her from any ants which might be around. But she rather wished, now, that he hadn't. His skin was tanned, smooth and hairless and she wanted to kiss it so badly. To lift the dark silken hair off his nape and plant a kiss there. Run a little trail of burning kisses down the humped ridges of his vertebrae with her lips. Perhaps . . .

He turned to look at her, and she knew she must have gone beetroot red. Surely he'd been able to read her thoughts. They'd probably been tattooed on her face for anyone to read. Her heart lurched as his green eyes darkened to almost black. Yes. He'd known what she was thinking all right. And as if in answer, he was turning to face her. He moved almost reluctantly, as if he resented the pull of their bodies, the dual magnetism which seemed to be perpetually drawing them together.

He was such a strange man. A man with secrets. A man who ran dark and deep. Perhaps too deep for her? She was out of her depth, and knew it. She should stop it. She should stop all this right now.

Dane reached out one long, strong hand and pushed the dark hair back from her face. His fingers seemed to burn four spots into her cheek as he leaned towards her, pulling her face to his, his eyes narrowing, glowing cat-green in the shade.

Persis drew in a quick breath, then moaned a little as their lips met. She felt his hands rise from her waist to gently cup one breast. She also felt herself burgeoning to meet him, and she raised one knee in a literal knee-jerk reaction. It was as if she was being touched for the first time.

She opened her eyes, confused pools of grey, asking she knew not what.

Dane stared down at her. 'Are you sure you want this?' he asked huskily.

And suddenly, somewhere close by, a child laughed jarringly. Instantly, Persis jerked upright. What was she thinking? They were in a public place, for pity's sake. All her middle-class upbringing came rushing to the fore. True, they were well hidden, but what if that child had come running in here? She might have been naked and in his arms by then.

Because she knew only too well what her answer to his question had been.

Of course she wanted this. She wanted this more than anything else in the world. But already his face was a closed and shuttered mask. Surely she'd seen something there, just a few moments ago. Hadn't she? He'd wanted her too. She knew it.

And yet there was still something else. Something harsh standing between them, keeping them apart. At first, she'd thought it was her own inexperience, her own timidity. But now she knew it was not that. Passion would always find a way.

So what was it? Oh, how she wished she knew!

He stood up and held out his hand to help her to her feet, then picked up his shirt and slipped it over that tanned, muscled flesh that had so captivated her. Dane Culver. Strong, good-looking, a man who mined opals and ore. A man who wanted her. A man who was surely used to taking what he wanted.

So why did he look at her with his wonderful green eyes so carefully veiled?

CHAPTER FIVE

The Indian Pacific *and Port Augusta*

The train left Adelaide at six that evening and passed back up the same stretch of track, north, towards the junction at Crystal Brook. In her cabin, Persis reached listlessly for her brochure on Port Augusta, which, according to the tourist board, was the 'crossroads of Australia'.

While just a few days ago the idea of exploring the Arid Lands, with some of the most highly evolved life systems on earth, not to mention a habitat as biologically sustainable as any rainforest, would have intrigued and engrossed her, now she found herself quickly tossing aside the glossy magazine and sighing heavily.

Her mind was too chaotic to settle on anything other than Dane Culver. What was wrong with him? Or her? Something was, she was sure of it. She leaned back in her chair with yet another massive sigh, watching the never-ending panorama that was Australia flash by her window. Soon she would be arriving at the quiet waterways at the head of Spencer Gulf, close to the spectacular Flinders Ranges, but what did that matter if she couldn't enjoy it? Her holiday, so looked forward to during her dreary days in hospital, was fast turning into a minefield.

She had to sort herself out. It wasn't like her to be emotionally messy — or any kind of messy, come to that. An only child, she'd always been neat and tidy and had worked hard at school to get good grades. These she had built upon, to gain a respectable degree in the history of fine art. Her father, dead now for several years, had left her enough money to go into partnership in the Woodstock gallery, and so, in many ways, she'd always had her eye on the ball, always been capable. Not even her mystery illness had been allowed to defeat her. She'd always stayed optimistic, enduring the enervating weakness and physical infirmity with a stoicism which had surprised even herself, just a little.

Perhaps she just had a lacklustre personality, Persis mused, beginning to feel depressed. She'd certainly never been tempted by the dashing and dangerous allure of too-fast living. She drank, but only moderately. Didn't smoke and had never indulged in drugs, even mild ones, not even at university, when it had seemed to be almost compulsory. Now, at the age of twenty-five, she'd come to the conclusion that she had found an ideal, if not exciting, equilibrium. Not even her abortive relationship with Rob had permanently crushed her sense of self or her idea of her place in the world.

But now! Now she was totally confused. In the space of a few days, a man she hardly knew had turned her world, and herself, upside down. It had to stop! Persis raised a hand to brush back her dark locks of hair and tried to put things in perspective. Perhaps it would help.

First, they had met at the café in Sydney, and right from the start, things had been weird. No other man had affected her the way he had. She'd sensed him watching her with an instinctive feeling which was utterly new to her. Feminine intuition, maybe? She hadn't given it much thought until now. But even before they'd spoken, she'd mentally labelled Dane as a predator, a wolf, a man on the make. The kind she usually avoided like the plague. But not this man and not this time. Why not? Fretfully, she searched her mind but could come to no logical conclusion. Scrap logic then. Perhaps logic had nothing to do with it. Try chemistry. Her mind went back to when she'd stumbled after leaving the table and he'd caught her. Her body had reacted like a live wire. And again, that was new. Her relationship with Rob had been one of long standing and had built itself up out of friendship and respect — and it had failed dismally. So perhaps those exponents of passion and spontaneity had it right after all. Could all this simply be put down to love at first sight? Or even lust at first sight? Had the spark she'd felt when Dane Culver had touched her been the catalyst for all this turmoil? Almost certainly. And yet, there was still something else.

During their memorable race up into the mountains, she'd sensed herself coming alive. She'd put it down to her recovery from her illness, but could it have been more than that? And Dane. How was he feeling about all this? What was *he* thinking? Was she alone in this voyage of discovery, or did she have a fellow passenger?

Persis closed her eyes for a moment, recalling his face. Alert. Watchful. Sometimes, it seemed, he looked at her as if he hated her. No. Not hated her. But distrusted her. Disliked her, perhaps? And yet, when they'd kissed at the Botanical Gardens, he hadn't disliked her then — far from it! Even she, mere novice that she was in all matters of love and lust, knew that much. And besides, if he disliked her, why did he keep seeking out her company? No, she wasn't wrong about something being off. Her instincts, newly awakened though they might be, weren't letting her down. There was definitely something odd going on here.

The question was — what should she do about it? Her old self had no problems answering that. She could hear it now, that cool, calm, reasonable voice, deep inside herself. *Back away. Play safe. Be cool the next time you see him. Be polite, but make it clear you're not willing to play whatever game it is he's masterminding.*

And she could do that, couldn't she? Simply back off, embrace her holiday, concentrate on enjoying the sights and sounds and minutiae of Australia. She glanced at the brochure lying beside her, reading a few lines about the Nukunu tribe, whose traditional territory she would soon be entering.

But already her old self was losing ground.

Why was it necessary to play safe? What did she have to lose, after all? Wasn't it more important to find out what she could gain? Immediately her body leapt and into her mind flashed the image of green eyes, mysterious, cool, but burning with promise. She could gain a lover, that was for sure. One, moreover, who could teach her what passion really was. Was that so terrible?

Ah, but what else might she gain? A heartache which wasn't as easily overcome as a stubborn virus? She had only to think of Dane Culver to know that here was a man who could do many things to her. And not all of them pleasant. She was in over her head, that was the plain and simple truth of it. So, it was either sink or swim time.

And Persis was tired of sinking. It was time she learned a nice, crisp overarm crawl. Or even a smooth-action breaststroke!

* * *

After dining aboard, Avery was glad to get off the train at a quarter past ten that night. Though the cabins were comfortable, and with the vastness of the landscape rolling past the window there was certainly no sense of claustrophobia, he was glad to be rid of the sensation of perpetual movement for a few hours. He wondered if he should include a warning about that in the final brochure, but shelved making a decision about it until later.

He snared a taxi for himself and Rayne, unknowingly following Persis and Dane to the same hotel — the Westside off the main highway, situated beside a quiet beach. The room he was shown to was spacious and predominately white, with an old-fashioned iron headboard and a matching one at the foot of the bed. It was painted white, black and gold. Nice. He wished, though, that it had one additional feature; namely, Rayne Fletcher stretched saucily nude and lying smack bang in the middle of it.

As he pulled off his shoes and headed for the shower, he wondered if he should have made the first move by now. Perhaps she was wondering what he was waiting for? On the other hand, she was hardly the shy and retiring type. If she'd wanted to, she'd have had no problem in leading him to her bed by now — probably by holding on tightly to a certain area of his anatomy, thus giving him no other option but to go with her or suffer castration! He laughed to himself under the shower and decided that the best things in life really were worth waiting for.

And Rayne was definitely one of the best things that had happened to him in some time.

Born poor, he'd always had a fire in his belly to make something of himself. To be in a position, one day, to buy himself a foreign sports car, to wear designer clothes, to go on holidays in places which he'd only seen on the telly before. And now he could do all of those things.

His first major purchase, however, had been a modest but well-built detached house on the outskirts of Wolverhampton — not for himself, but for his mum, dad and his sister Katy, who'd still been living at home at the time. He himself had been happier with a rented flat in London, where Cloud Nine had its base.

He'd worked like a dog for the last ten years and now, he supposed by anyone's standards, he'd made it. So why had it taken Rayne Fletcher to make him realize how empty his life had been before? Oh, he'd had female companionship — in plenty — during those working business trips to check out the beaches in the Caribbean, the wildlife on the safaris, and the standard of accommodation in the more far-off places. But now they all felt somehow hollow and pointless.

He turned off the shower and towelled himself dry, walked naked to the mirror and looked thoughtfully at his reflection. He saw a fit, reasonably good-looking thirty-three-year-old man looking back at him. A rich and successful man — a working-class boy made good. He'd swum in the shark-infested waters of the city-slicker types and had come out on top. He was the hero of his family. He had only to pick up his little black book, select a name, and be assured of the companionship of any number of beautiful, sophisticated, worldly-wise women. He was a success, no doubt about it. Everything had gone according to plan.

And now he'd met Rayne Fletcher. Another beautiful, sophisticated, worldly-wise woman.

Ah, but she was different. She had something more to offer. And he, let's face it, he thought, wrinkling his face in the mirror, was ready to accept it. Was it time to settle down? Raise a family? Had he at last found a woman with whom he was ready to do all that? Yes. Probably. There was all of that. And she made him laugh; she made him sing. She made him glad that he was still young, and good-looking, and fit.

Avery grinned at himself and went to bed. He supposed he should be terrified at what was happening to him. But he wasn't. Falling in love, he was discovering, wasn't so hard — or so bad — after all. Modern male mythology on the subject be damned!

* * *

In her room, Rayne carefully put the scrap of paper with his address and signature on it into an envelope and addressed it to her firm in London. Tomorrow she'd FedEx it as fast as possible back home with the request that the handwriting expert be let loose on it. Nowadays, it was not just the shape of the lettering which could determine its authenticity, she knew, because there were many other variables to be taken into account too. Like the amount of times the pen was lifted on and off the paper. And the depth, equalling the force, with which the pen was wielded on certain letters. She'd done a course in handwriting analysis once, and knew that, even though the best forgers could make writing look identical to someone else's, it was all but impossible to write in the same *way* as another.

She sighed and slipped off her clothes, settling into the cool sheets and wondering why she felt so miserable. Soon she'd have confirmation that it was Avery's signature on those insurance documents. The arson was already proved. They just needed to find the arsonist Avery had hired and then they'd strike. They might call in the cops, but then again, her boss might not. If Avery backed off and agreed to void the claim, he might just do a deal whereby Avery needn't end up in jail. Insurance companies weren't there to help the police — only to safeguard their profits! So there was no need to worry that what she was doing would lead Avery McLeod straight to Wormwood Scrubs, necessarily.

So why was she lying here awake and worrying? Dammit!

* * *

The next morning, Avery was down to breakfast first. The dining room was slowly filling, and his eyes lingered for a while on a tall, leggy brunette as she paused in the doorway. He'd seen her before on the train, and supposed she was doing a tour very similar to his own. She had lovely grey eyes, he noticed, and the pure white dress she was wearing showed off to perfection the golden tan she was fast acquiring. She was as slender as a willow reed (too skinny for his tastes) and as he watched her he saw, off to his left, a man rise slowly to his feet in greeting.

Avery smiled. No way a girl like that would be on her own for long, of course.

He saw the woman acknowledge the man and something flickered across her face. It was an intriguing expression, one which aroused his curiosity instantly. He'd never seen a woman look at a man quite like that before. He watched her weave her way with effortless grace through the tables towards her mark, who was watching her approach with hooded eyes.

Avery wondered what he could possibly be thinking. His face belonged on someone about to play a game of poker with big stakes, and not at all on the face of a man watching a beautiful woman approach him.

Now he was thoroughly intrigued.

'Earth to Major Tom. Can you hear me, Major Tom?' Rayne's hand, her fingertips painted a bright scarlet to go with the short scarlet sundress she was wearing, waved in front of his face, and he blinked, grinning guiltily. 'Sorry. I was people watching,' he apologized, and nodded towards the other couple.

'Oh yes. I love doing that too. Let's see — I've spoken to her on the train. She's English too.' Rayne took the seat opposite him, the letter in her handbag feeling as if it was burning a hole through the leather.

Avery, the other couple quickly forgotten now that Rayne was here, looked at her openly, admiring the golden sheen of her curls, her petite but curvaceous figure, and the candour in her big blue eyes. 'Mornin', gorgeous,' he said softly.

Rayne gulped. Did he have to look at her like that? As if he was so damned pleased to see her? Recognizing her anger for what it was — incipient guilt — she turned her dismayed gaze quickly to the menu. Damn it, what was with her today? She'd done this job, and very successfully too, for over four years now. A major promotion was within her grasp. She had plans. And they didn't include a charming, good-looking ne'er-do-well called Avery bloody McLeod.

'The Illawarra plums look good,' she murmured.

From his table, Felix Barstow watched them, and didn't like what he saw. The blonde was antsy, and definitely acting like a cat on a hot tin roof. That could only mean one thing. The silly little cow was falling for him. Why the hell did insurance companies hire women anyway?

Felix, a woman-hater of many years standing, sighed and ordered the herb omelette with fried tomatoes, and lemon myrtle tea.

And firmly turned his thoughts to plan B.

Within a day or so, they'd change trains and head for that famous middle-of-nowhere place, Alice Springs. Alice

Springs, where there was nothing for thousands of miles wherever you looked. One of the most deserted, desolate spots in the world. Unforgiving heat. Merciless sun. Desiccating air. The kind of place where careless tourists could easily get lost. Disappear. Even die.

* * *

After visiting the Wadlata Outback Centre and having fun with the interactive displays, Rayne managed to slip away to post her letter and, feeling more glum than ever, rejoined Avery to check out the 'Flying Doctor'. No visit to Australia, she agreed, would be complete without it. It was, they learned, one of fourteen bases in the country, and as well as providing emergency medical services, also ran a routine monthly visiting service to people in remote and isolated areas. The smart white planes with the red logo on the tail looked primed for action, but with little else to see, they quickly returned to town.

'Let's hit the beach,' Avery said, glad when her eyes lit up. 'Sorry, this hasn't been much fun for you, has it? What if I pay you a consultancy fee?'

Rayne's eyes narrowed dangerously. What was this? A bribe? Had he cottoned on to her? 'What do you mean?' she said suspiciously. 'I don't want your money,' she added, her voice tight and dangerous all of a sudden.

Avery's eyes widened for a moment, then he stepped back, holding up two hands and making a cross with his index fingers. 'Back, keep back, vampire of the darkness,' he said, his voice all a-quiver. 'All I meant was, you're doing a job of work for me by being an unpaid guinea pig and getting dragged to practically every tourist trap this side of the Barrier Reef. So I just thought that it would only be fair if I paid you for your time — the going rate of one of our reps, for instance. I didn't mean to raise your considerable hackles. Honest.'

Rayne felt herself wilt with relief, then bit her lip. She was acting like an idiot — an ultra-sensitive idiot. She smiled ruefully. 'Sorry. You just touched me on the raw there.'

'No kidding?' Avery laughed. Then looked suddenly serious. 'Is it my money that's worrying you?' he asked softly.

Rayne blinked. Huh? *Huh?*

'I mean, for some women it can be a bit of an issue,' he said diffidently. 'You know — do I think they're gold-diggers. Will they be compromising their ethics and/or reputation if they let me pay not only for dinner but for everything else.'

Rayne began to laugh. 'Oh,' she said at last. Then, 'No. That's no problem. In fact, I positively like it that you're rich. And you can pay for everything from my drink to the price of my deck chair if you like. Race you!' she yelled, and she was off. 'Last one to the beach buys the beer.'

As Avery ran to his room to change, he was still grinning to himself. He never knew where he stood with Rayne. It was like trying to keep up with quicksilver.

In her room, Rayne changed into a minuscule, midnight-blue bikini, went to the mirror and ran a comb through her curls. Things were going great — right on course. Her eyes flickered as they looked back at her. Yeah. Right. Everything was just hunky-dory.

Suddenly, her eyes stopped flickering and went wide with shock. Slowly, still holding her own appalled gaze in the mirror, she sank to the stool in front of the dresser.

Oh shit.

Oh shit.

She was falling in love with him.

* * *

Persis looked up at the Water Tower Lookout. Built in 1882 to provide a pressure water supply for the town, it now provided a wonderful vantage point. Having already climbed the first few steps, Dane turned and looked down at her, then silently held out his hand. Without a word, she took it and began to climb wooden stairs. At the top, the town of Port Augusta, the Gulf and Flinders Range spread out before her from in front of the balcony like a gift. Bond Street and Mitchell Terrace faded, however, as Dane leaned beside her, looking out broodingly across to the ocean.

'Are you going home?' Persis asked softly, and saw him give a little start of surprise.

'What do you mean?'

'I mean, do you live in Perth? Is that why you're on the train? Only I just realised I've never asked you.'

Dane smiled. 'No. I'm on holiday.'

That's a lie, Persis thought instantly, but didn't say it aloud. What if she was wrong? But she knew she wasn't wrong. She just didn't want to know what he'd say if she spoke aloud. More lies? Or the truth. And if the truth, did she really want to know what it was? Her old self would have, but this was the new, improved Persis Canfield-Hope.

So she said nothing, but looked and waited.

'Tell me more about yourself,' Dane said. He noticed that a family were headed their way, probably to climb the tower as well, and, reaching for her hand, he led the way back down.

'There's nothing much to tell,' Persis said as they descended, but gave him a brief and accurate summary of her life as they walked around the gardens, then out into the town. Wandering aimlessly, they eventually found their way to the beach and a small jetty. A tall board with the heading 'Boats for Hire' dominated the end of the pier, and as they made their way towards it, she finally came to the end of her life's history.

She hadn't once mentioned Rob. Dane knew she'd been engaged from their earlier conversation, when she'd so bluntly questioned him about his own marital status, but aside from that there was simply nothing else to say about Rob anymore.

'And so, here I am,' she finished. Then took a deep breath, summoned up all her courage, and added, 'With you.'

Beside her, she sensed his head swing sharply towards her. 'Yes,' he said, so quietly she almost didn't hear him.

'With me,' he repeated softly. He knew what she was asking him, of course. But how could he answer?

'Would you like a trip out to sea?' he said instead, nodding towards one of the boats. It was one of the bigger ones for hire, with a small deck and simple boathouse. 'I know how to use one of these. We could hug the coastline for a few miles, see if there's any friendly marine wildlife about?'

Persis nodded. 'Sounds wonderful,' she said neutrally. So he wasn't going to answer her. Now what should she do?

* * *

It was hot and bright out on the ocean. Persis reached for her sunglasses and slipped them over her nose, and watched Dane thoughtfully as he steered them expertly out to sea. Gulls and other sea birds cried and called around her. The ocean itself was calm, and the boat, not very powerful, had a smooth action.

She closed her eyes.

She was on the other side of the world, in a small boat on a mighty ocean, with a man who excited and intrigued her. Her life was her own. She owed nothing to anybody. And suddenly, she knew exactly what she was going to do. Laying out a long beach towel, Persis took off her dark glasses, then reached out to undo the buttons of her sundress. It was a simple garment, loose and cool, and it slithered down her arms, over her waist, and pooled about her feet with a mere whisper.

But he heard it.

Turning his head, his green eyes widened then softened as she shyly turned her naked back to him before quickly lying down on the towel. For a few minutes, she kept her hands over her breasts, then turned onto her stomach and lay with her cheek pressed to her forearms.

Mata Hari she definitely wasn't. If he didn't do something soon, she'd feel a right fool. After all, she could hardly make things more clear, could she?

She felt the boat power back, then idle. Then the engine was turned off and the silence was almost absolute. Slowly she became aware of the quiet lap of the waves against the boat, and looked up as he dropped the anchor. He checked something on the instrument panel of the boat, and then turned towards her. She closed her eyes quickly, instinctively, like a tortoise ducking back into its shell. But in her case, her shell consisted of a pair of plain white briefs, and nothing else. She couldn't remember feeling more vulnerable — or defiant — in her life before.

She felt him stretch out beside her and tensed. Was she really up for this? Did she underst— She gasped as she felt his lips touch her back, low down, in the tender hollow where her spine dipped and then curved upwards to meet her buttocks. He kissed her again, following the line of her spine until his lips were between her shoulder blades. Instantly, against the warmth of the towel and the hard decking beneath, she felt her nipples harden and begin to tingle.

She dragged in a rather ragged breath. She should do something. Say something. 'I'll probably not be very good at this,' she warned huskily. Then froze. Had she really *said* that? She groaned, not quite audibly, and felt her face flush with shame.

Dane swallowed hard. Somehow, he'd already known that she was not the kind who enjoyed easy affairs and no-strings-attached rolls in the hay. He'd already sensed that this was probably one of the hardest things she'd ever done.

So why had she done it?

But, in truth, he knew the answer to that as well — although he wished he didn't. Wished instead that he could believe the half-hearted little voice in the back of his head which insisted that this was all so much hogwash. A trick — and what's more, one of the oldest in the book. But in his heart he knew that simply wasn't true. However much he might hope differently, he was not being played for a sucker. And the ramifications of that would have to be dealt with at some point.

'Persis,' he said softly, insistently, and after a moment, she raised her head and looked at him.

'I love you,' he said cautiously, and listened to himself, mostly for evidence of a denial. A snicker. A shamefaced acknowledgement of ham acting.

But nothing came.

'I love you,' he said again, more strongly this time, and knew that he meant it.

For one awful moment Persis felt her eyes fill with tears, and quickly blinked them away. Don't let her start howling now! 'Oh,' she said gruffly. She hadn't expected that. Sex was what she'd expected. A blow for her personal liberty, perhaps. Not this unexpected declaration.

He lowered his head to hers and kissed her lips, bare of lipstick and soft as cushions. When he lifted his head, she changed her somewhat awkward position, rolling onto one side. With her elbow bent on the towel, she cupped her chin in the palm of her hand, watching nervously as his eyes travelled down to her breasts, then back up again.

'You're beautiful,' he said, almost perfunctorily. As if it were a given.

'Don't you want me?' she asked, surprised.

Dane smiled, a slightly twisted smile. It made him look both breathtakingly handsome and heart-stoppingly ferocious at the same time. Her body began to turn liquid. 'Oh yes,' he said harshly. 'I want you all right.'

And proceeded to show her just how much. In a second he was moving over her, pressing her shoulders onto the deck, at the same time pulling his T-shirt over his head. It mussed his dark hair as it cleared his head, leaving exposed the deep, tanned expanse of his chest. His skin felt hot as it pressed against hers and his lips, descending on hers like a marauder, gave way to the hot, knowing thrust of his tongue.

Persis moaned, both helpless and thrilled. His hands and his hot knowing fingers moved from the tender curves of her breasts down to her waist, then one slipped to move between her legs, which fell open at his command. His finger ran cunningly and knowingly across the ridges it found there, making her squirm and shake.

His lips left hers, trailing a moist, sensation-creating line between her breasts, then his tongue was dipping into her navel, as if burrowing for treasure, and making her legs thrash helplessly against the deck. Then he moved lower, his dark head moving to between her thighs, until his mouth was pressed hard against the white cotton of her briefs, his tongue hot and firm against the hotness of her feminine core. His hands tore the briefs down, dragging them over her ankles and tossing them onto the deck.

She wondered, idly, if they'd slither down and fall into the sea. And didn't care if they did.

Firmly gripping each ankle, he lifted her trembling legs and she felt her calves being looped over each of his shoulders. She looked up just in time to see his dark head dip between her thighs and catch a glitter of cat-green, half-closed eyes as their gaze met for a microsecond. And then she screamed, a clear, wonderful, ecstatic cry which ricocheted off the water and around and around in her head. His tongue was remorseless, his lips and teeth a nibbling torment as he pushed her higher and higher, his hands strong and firm on her hips as she writhed and bucked, cursing his name over and over.

Later, a long time later, his face was above hers and she opened her eyes. She felt him nudging her thighs apart, his eyes locking onto hers. And then he moved into her, a long, hard, smooth slide which made her cry out, almost in pain, but not quite. She knew she was clinging to him, her nails clawing at his back and shoulders. Knew that her voice was becoming hoarse with all her cries. Sensed every muscle and sinew dancing to his time, her legs locked around his waist, her heels digging into the hard length of his thighs, and her heart crashing like some mighty engine deep in her breast.

His hair was damp now with sweat, his face as taut as a bow string, his eyes a green fire glowing in the dark tan of his face. His voice, groaning her name, had her heart soaring with pride. It wasn't just her! She was doing this to him, too.

The intensity of the moment was something utterly new to her. She saw his face begin to contort, felt her own body buck wildly as if touched by electricity, and then she was above and beyond all that, and soaring free.

She felt his collapsing weight and cradled his head tenderly. Her eyes closed.

So this was it. And it was wonderful — surely well worth any risk or sacrifice. Whatever Dane Culver wanted, as far as Persis was concerned, Dane Culver could have it.

CHAPTER SIX

The Indian Pacific, *Tarcoola and* The Ghan

Persis looked out the window as the *Indian Pacific* train, which was already beginning to feel like a home away from home, pulled into Tarcoola station. A quick glance at her watch showed her that it was dead on time. When she alighted, making sure that she had her well-packed cases of carefully selected belongings with her, the station clock was just about to strike eleven o'clock at night.

For some reason she had yet to fathom, *The Ghan*, the train which would take her to Alice Springs, didn't leave until 4.23 a.m. She hoped Tarcoola was a friendly town with a couple of all-night bars. Or maybe she should take a room for a few hours? She'd wait and see what Dane wanted. She saw him almost as she formed the words in her mind, and as she watched him turn his head, obviously searching the busy platform for her, she experienced one of life's 'moments'.

All around her was the sound of a busy train station. As well as the twangy accents of Australians, there were also the more fast-paced, staccato words of East Asia. The air, even at night, felt hot and smelt dusty. People moved all around her, anxious to be gone, to find their connections, to meet relatives. Outside, in the dark, strange and fabulous animals with mysterious, evocative names lurked in the desert. Wombats. Bandicoots, perhaps? All sorts of possums, maybe even a Tasmanian devil. Or did you only get those on Tasmania itself, Australia's smallest state and offshore island? From the darkness, history called — Aborigines on walkabout, exploring the Dreamtime. And all this under the watchful eye of the Southern Cross. Amidst it all, she stood alone, watching the man she'd come to love seeking her out.

His dark brown hair was given a red-gold sheen by the overhead lamplight, and as his eyes finally found and locked onto hers she could sense the tension in him. Her heart lost a beat and found it again, her breath likewise catching in her breast. Time seemed to stand still, and she knew, just *knew*, that if she lived to be ninety, she would be able to recall this moment in utter clarity whenever she wanted to summon it up.

But like all 'moments' it was gone almost before she could examine it. He began to move towards her and she noticed how people moved out of his way instinctively, as if not wanting to impede him. He walked with that easy ranging lope she was beginning to understand, as if it were part of the man. His shirt was sweat-damp under his arms and no doubt between his shoulder blades as well, his hair damp against his temples and forehead. He was magnificent. And, she realized, with a thrill of ownership and disbelief, nearly every woman on the platform was also watching him, admiring and wondering.

And he was coming for *her*.

It wasn't something that she had ever thought would happen to her, back home, safe in her old little world. She had Woodstock and the gallery, her mother, her friends. But that felt like a whole lifetime ago now.

Now she had *him*. And this strange country. And her new self.

Persis let out her breath in a long low sigh as he drew near her and she smiled to hide a sudden sense of panic. So they were lovers. But what would happen now? How long could any of this last?

'You look tired,' he said softly. 'I've got a room at an inn near here. What say we catch a few hours' sleep?'

Persis did, in fact, feel tired. But did he really mean sleep? Or something else? 'All right,' she said softly, and watched him as he bent to pick up her luggage. His own knapsack was slung across his shoulders already, the straps tight against his shirt, exposing the outline of the bulging muscles in his arms and chest.

The inn was simple and modest, and consisted of one room with a double bed. Persis used the bathroom first, brushing her teeth then combing out her hair, and then looked at her single nightdress, a simple plain white affair, with some dismay. Knee-length, with a pretty scalloped neckline and hemline, it was fine for sleeping in, but it was hardly the black silk baby-doll one would choose to entertain a new lover. But then, when she'd packed it, she'd had no idea she'd be wearing it for a man like Dane Culver. Well, it was either that or go into the bedroom stark naked. And not even the new and improved Persis Canfield-Hope had the gumption for that quite yet!

She opened the door, unaware that the light from the bathroom behind her showed the shape of her slender form through the thin white cotton. Or that the innocent simplicity of it made her look more breathtakingly lovely than any baby-doll nightie could have managed.

Dane, who was sat on the end of the bed, having taken off his shoes and socks, looked up at her and felt his body go rigid in shock. Stupid, of course, considering what they'd already done on the boat — which had been far more intense. And, after what he'd learned from that, he really had no excuse now for being bowled over by her. But he was. For the first time in his life, he felt unsure what to do next.

Persis looked uncertainly from him to the bed, then walked across, wordlessly slipped back the sheets and slithered inside. Dane, on legs which felt distinctly unsure at the knees, walked into the bathroom without a word. There, he reached for his razor and shaved, meeting his gaze without flinching.

All right, so he was in love with the girl. That was bad enough. And she, if his own instincts could be believed, wasn't exactly immune to him either. But where did that leave them exactly? Until this situation with *Iris* was sorted out, there was nothing to be done about it.

Angrily, he brushed his teeth, turned off the light, and walked into the room. For a while he stood looking down at her thoughtfully, and a sudden tenderness tugged at his Adam's apple, making him swallow convulsively.

She'd turned off the lamp on her side of the bed and was lying curled up in a foetal position, her eyes tightly shut. But she wasn't asleep. He sighed, moved to his own side of the bed, turned off the lamp and lay staring at the ceiling. He knew he would never be able to sleep, but he also knew that she needed to.

His report from the PI firm he'd used had come through for him, telling him that Persis Canfield-Hope had indeed been hospitalized, although the cause had been something of a mystery. The agent hadn't been able to establish what her exact diagnosis had been, but *had* been able to confirm that whatever she suffered from, although it had proved nasty and upsetting, wasn't believed to be either terminal or dangerous. When he'd got the email report a few hours ago he'd felt almost sick with relief. But still, she needed time to recuperate. He would have to take things slow and easy, if only to ensure her continuing good health.

He turned and pulled her into his arms, cradling her head on his shoulder. Absently he began to stroke her long, dark locks. 'Go to sleep,' he said softly, and kissed her temple.

Persis closed her eyes and sighed gently. It felt good where she was. Safe. Warm. Comfortable. And the fact that he wasn't going to make love to her after all, strangely, felt right.

As if she could trust him.

Dane Culver continued to stare at the ceiling long after her slow even breaths told him she was asleep.

* * *

'You know, we'd really need to figure out something about this stopover,' Avery said. They were both at a bar, eating peanuts and drinking Aussie beer, with Rayne swinging her legs from side to side on her stool, much to the delight of the boggle-eyed barman.

She nodded. 'Yeah, it's a bit of a drag,' she agreed. She was wearing very short shorts in pale lemon, with a matching lemon, white and mint-green top. She reached for a peanut, popped it into her mouth, and looked at the telly.

It was showing coverage of a cricket match. What else? 'Mind you,' she said, looking around the smoke-palled, less-than-salubrious small-town bar, 'I quite like a touch of the low-life now and then. Provided I have interesting company, that is.'

Avery glanced across at her and grinned. 'Why, I do believe that was a compliment.'

Rayne gurgled into her beer. 'Don't let it go to your head,' she advised, and sighed wistfully. She was feeling fey tonight. No two ways about it. She knew these reckless moods of hers — they usually presaged no good. Luckily, she wasn't prey to them often, but when she was . . . things tended to happen.

Perhaps it was because the train had gone, leaving without her and giving her a sense of rather pleasant abandonment. It was the early hours of the morning, and she had nothing to do and nowhere to go, except talk to Avery McLeod. Flirt with Avery McLeod. Stalk Avery McLeod.

Want Avery McLeod.

She eyed him as she tossed back her beer, cold from the fridge and straight from the bottle. What was it about him that gave her such grief? OK, he was good-looking, but she'd known movie-star handsome men before. He was wealthy, which was always nice, but in her business, she regularly flirted with men who were damned near billionaires. Some even asked her out, but her boss didn't like her to say yes.

Not that she hadn't *said* yes a few times.

So what had made her go and fall in love with a crook? If he was a crook. But maybe he wasn't.

'So how come you called your business Cloud Nine?' she asked, looking up as the crowd on the television screen went wild. Someone must have scored a goal or something. Or whatever the hell it was they did in cricket.

'That was a pun on my partner's name. Greg Nones. Nones, meaning Nine.' He shrugged. 'And we thought it would make for some great slogans — you know, take a holiday with us and you'll be on Cloud Nine. Two weeks with us and get that Cloud Nine feeling for the rest of the year. You name it, the advertising boffins thought of it.'

Rayne laughed. 'From the look on your face, you don't seem too impressed.'

Avery shrugged. 'Oh, I'm just getting restless, I guess. Greg and I don't get along — we never have. I'm not sure I completely trust him.'

'Oh?' Rayne said, her pulse rate climbing just a little. 'Anything specific?'

'Nah. Let's just say I caught him out in some creative book-keeping once or twice. And he likes to sail too close to the wind for my preference. When we first started out, and it was all his money, then fair enough, I suppose. But now it's different. I've got over eight years of my life invested in Cloud Nine; I helped build it, and now I'm a major shareholder.' He shrugged. 'Greg doesn't like hard work, so he's become more or less a sleeping partner. Frankly, I can do without him.'

'You've been falling out?' Rayne suggested, hoping her eyes weren't glowing. Because what if they were on the wrong track after all? Right firm, right scam, but wrong man? From all she was hearing, Greg Nones was a far more likely candidate to try an insurance scam than Avery. A work-shy rich kid with a gambling problem, he was just the sort of cocky lad who *might* just think he could get away with it. As if the world, and insurance companies like her own in particular, owed him a living.

Or was she just kidding herself here? Because she wanted this guy sat next to her to be fair game, was she just looking for a way to give herself the green light to take him to her bed, or was she really on to something?

'You could say that,' Avery laughed, in answer to her question. 'Oh hell, I can't see me and Greg staying together much longer anyway. I want him out, and he knows it. And the board knows I'm really the guts behind the outfit now. As soon as I can sort some serious financing out with the banks, Greg will be voted out, and I suppose he knows that too.'

Rayne nodded. That was good. Very good. Because what might a man who knew he was going to get his marching orders think about it? Especially if he was a spoilt little rich twerp, someone to whom the usual laws never applied. Might he not just come up with such a scheme as the burning down of Littledore Manor? Rayne slowly swivelled round on her stool, trying to tell herself to keep cool. It might just be so much pie in the sky. Wanting Greg Nones to be the real villain of the piece didn't make him so. But she could get her PA back at the firm to start making enquiries, couldn't she? It never hurt to have another bird in another bush, after all.

'So, will you be thinking of expanding? Once you've got Cloud Nine to yourself?' she asked craftily. 'You know, go into the hotel business, mass tourism, package holidays on a bigger scale?'

Avery dragged his glance from her tanned legs and shook his head. 'Nah. I leave the big tourist packages to the big boys. Speciality holidays, that's what I'm interested in. Keep it relatively small and you can give a customer personal service and go in for the unusual stuff. That's where you can still pull some surprises. I had a guy last year who wanted to travel halfway up Mount Everest. Not climb it, just "sort of be there", as he put it. And I arranged it. Had to go through all sorts of channels, as you can imagine. Cost the guy a fortune, but he was happy. And as for hotels, forget it. The field's a landmine.'

Rayne, who was in the act of reaching for another peanut, froze for a moment, then carried smoothly on, reaching for the salty nut. She looked at him as she popped it into her mouth. 'So you wouldn't be interested in, say, taking an old house, a bit run-down, and turning it into a swanky spot for Cloud Nine patrons?' she asked, chewing slowly.

Avery laughed. 'Hell, no. What would I want to do that for? I get a couple come into the shop who want a romantic honeymoon spot for two, I log onto the net and I've got my pick of thousands of hotels. Why go through the hassle of owning one, and all the headaches which come with it? For a start, a hotel has to constantly hit its quota. The number of guests falls below that quota, and there's your profit gone, right then and there. Why bother?'

Why bother indeed, Rayne thought, beginning to grin. Because he obviously meant what he said. She'd have bet her last month's salary on it. But that still didn't mean he didn't buy Littledore Manor with the express purpose of burning it down. It only meant he'd never intended it to be a viable concern in the first place.

Still.

Oh hell, Rayne thought. She was going to end up with this man, one way or the other. She just knew it. Who knows, perhaps he wasn't a crook. Perhaps she'd get him out of her system before she had to shop him. Perhaps she'd get her damned stupid heart broken. What was the point of worrying which it was?

Oh yes, no doubt about it. She was feeling fey tonight.

* * *

The light of dawn was turning into the light of day when *The Ghan* pulled into Tarcoola station, with its dark green engine pulling a long train of silver carriages. It wasn't due to leave until 4.23, but already everybody bound for Alice Springs was there on the platform, waiting for it.

Smaller than the express she was used to, Persis watched it pull in and hoped, while on board, she'd be able to catch a glimpse or two of Australia's wild camel population. Up until 1929, she knew, camels had been the lifeline of Alice Springs, as they'd been the only way of ferrying goods, food and news of the outside world to 'The Alice', as the locals called it. Nowadays, the camels, turned loose, had become a success story.

For the next twenty hours, she knew, she was in for a treat, seeing some of Australia's most stunning scenery — especially the MacDonnell Ranges of Alice Springs. And, even better, she'd have Dane to watch it with her. Would there be an observation deck on the train? Could she watch, holding Dane's hand, as they approached Alice Springs with its occasionally flowing Todd River, while the train passed through the Heavitree Gap?

She glanced around as the train pulled to a smooth halt in front of her, and people began to board.

Dane had gone momentarily missing, but then she saw him at the phone booth. He saw her, and nodded as she pointed to the train, picked up her cases and climbed aboard. It felt good to be getting her full upper-body strength back, and the independence which went with it. A helpful steward inside took her ticket, however, and carried her case to her first-class single cabin. She hoped Dane's own would be nearby. Perhaps she should see about getting her single ticket exchanged for a double one? Or would Dane prefer to keep some of his privacy?

She wished she knew what he'd want. It seemed to her ominous that she didn't. As if she should know him by now. But that was absurd. Sleeping for a few hours in a man's arms, and making love to him once, didn't make her privy to his every thought and want. And wasn't that half the fun, anyway? The whole getting-to-know-you thing, surely, was in many ways more important than mere physical gratification.

She only wished she knew rather more about him than she did!

Dane hung up the phone and turned from the booth, staring at the train. The situation in Perth was slowly getting worse. Soon, he knew, things would come to a head. And by then, he'd have to have fulfilled his promise.

Which meant getting his hands on that damned diary.

* * *

As Dane climbed on board the train, behind him, Felix Barstow waited until he was clear, then moved with some relief into the cooler interior of the train. He didn't like Australia. He didn't like the heat, the vast, never-ending nothingness, the creepy-crawlies or the people.

He'd be glad to get home. But first he had a little job to do.

It wasn't hard to find out where Avery McLeod's cabin was, and a quick look showed it still to be empty. Either the tourist operator hadn't boarded yet, or he'd been and stowed his stuff away and left it already. No doubt to go to the blonde insurance investigator's room. His lips twisted in a nasty smile as he surreptitiously glanced around, was reassured by the melee in the narrow corridors, and smoothly slid into Avery's cabin, firmly shutting the door behind him.

He glanced around in disapproval. Compact, neat, comfortable, but hardly a good spot for finding hiding places. He went to the tiny wardrobe, then pulled out a drawer. It was utterly empty, but he noticed a big haversack was stowed away under the chair. He glanced at it, then shook his head. No. No good planting the evidence there. McLeod might find it first.

He looked back at the empty drawer. It was no use putting it there, either. Unless . . . With a smile, Felix nipped back out onto the platform, bought a copy of the local paper and reboarded. The room was still vacant, and slipping the evidence into the drawer, he carefully laid out the copy of the newspaper over it. Good. Now all he had to do was wait. At some point Blondie was bound to search her mark's room, and this long stretch towards Alice Springs was the ideal time to do it.

Felix closed the drawer then patted it affectionately. And if she never did find it, so what? It was only a backup measure. If things went according to plan, she and her lover boy would never be leaving Alice Springs alive anyway.

* * *

Persis glanced up as the door opened and Dane looked in. 'Ready for lunch?' he asked.

Persis nodded. 'But I thought we could eat here. It'll be cosier than in one of the dining cars.'

Dane nodded. 'Sounds wonderful.' Then, casually, 'What's that you're reading?' As if he didn't know.

'Gran's diary,' Persis said, closing it up and putting it carelessly on the small window ledge. 'Have you managed to unpack all right? I'm only just getting used to it myself. Finally, I've got into the habit of putting all the overnight stuff and bare essentials on top,' she said, biting her lip and telling herself not to burble like an idiot. She watched as he pulled down the foldaway chair and sat opposite her. A small table could be pulled out for when they ordered lunch, and she fiddled with the handle as he dropped down opposite her.

He noticed the tell-tale nervous gesture and too-quick chit-chat, and sighed. He didn't like doing this to her. He wished, in that moment, that she was just a little harder, just a little less vulnerable. But then, he was in love with the woman. He'd feel guilty even if she had the hide of an elephant.

'So, tell me more about your grandmother,' he said, for the first time in his life managing to think about Angela Canfield-Hope without wanting to spit her name out like poison. This girl was definitely mellowing him. Perhaps too much.

'Oh, she was marvellous,' Persis said, her face lighting up. At least this was something normal she could talk about. Although the last few days had been wonderful, they'd been intense, and her nerves had begun to let her know it. 'I was hoping I might find out more about her life here, but that'll have to wait until Kalgoorlie,' she said, missing the way he suddenly started and then narrowed his eyes.

'Kalgoorlie? Why there?' he asked gruffly.

'Oh, I think that's where she and her Walter C spent most of their time. I'm not sure, but I think that's where Iris might have been born. Or perhaps conceived. It's hard to tell from her diary. She was so secretive.'

Dane slowly leaned back against the wall and nodded. Kalgoorlie. It made sense. Back in those days, his grandfather had a load of mines in that town. Some being shut down, others being started up. They'd had some labour trouble too, back then, if he remembered right. He was sure that it had been between the wars. He remembered his father telling him that his grandfather had been away from home for months at a stretch sometimes. Maybe even a year. No doubt that was when Angela had got her hooks into him. Damn her, she must have tied the old man in knots to get him to give away the Iris Stone like he had.

'Wouldn't it be wonderful if I could find her? My Aunt Iris, I mean,' Persis said, as he watched her with those green, level, almost cold eyes. 'Kalgoorlie's not a big place, is it? We could probably find out about her from the hall of records or something.'

Dane shrugged. The hall of records would be no help to her at all. But he couldn't say so. Damn it, he felt like someone from one of those old legends. He stood on one side of a cliff, she on the other, with a raging, uncrossable sea between them. But he had no intention of flinging himself to a watery grave, or letting her do so either. No. In this legend, he was going to build a great big bridge, get the Iris Stone back where it belonged, and have the girl too. And the Canfield-Hopes could all go hang!

But what he needed now were some hard facts.

'Tell me, what have you been told about what happened when your grandmother got home?' he asked, in what he hoped was a nonchalant, only mildly interested tone.

'What do you mean?'

'Well where was she living?'

'I don't know. In Kensington, I think,' Persis said.

'Kensington? Isn't that one of the rich parts of the city?'

Persis laughed. 'So-so. Mind you, I don't know London that well myself. Everyone here seems to think that, because I'm a pom, I must know London like the back of my hand. The fact is, I've lived in Oxfordshire all my life. I can tell you as much about Oxford as you like.' She gave a pretty shrug which made him smile and also made him want to kiss her shoulders. But he had better keep his mind on the job at hand.

'So she must have returned from Oz with a fair bit of money then?' he probed, holding his breath.

'I don't think so,' Persis said, a little puzzled. Why was he asking her these kinds of questions? 'As far as I know, Gran's only money came from her parents. They weren't rich, but her father was the vicar of a fairly wealthy village, and I think her mother shared a reasonably large inheritance with her three sisters. Apart from that . . .' She again shrugged and held out her hands in a speaking gesture.

Dane felt himself relax. So Angela hadn't sold it then. It had been the one thing that really worried him. If it had been sold all those years ago, he'd never be able to trace it now. But the fact that it had never publicly surfaced had always led his family to believe that the Iris Stone must still be in the possession of the Canfield-Hope clan. And the fact that they'd never publicized it only meant that they knew damned well that they weren't entitled to it.

But Persis obviously had no idea where it was now. 'So, your great aunts probably told you all about your grandmother's exploits,' he said softly.

'Some,' she agreed, obviously wondering where all this was leading. But how the hell could he ask her if any of them might know about Angela's shameful secret, and yet still keep Persis in the dark?

'Did you see much of them?' he persisted carefully.

'No. Two of them died not long after Angela. The youngest went to America, but died a few years ago.'

Dane sighed. Dammit, could it be over there in the States after all? 'Did she have a family there? In America, I mean.'

'No. Just her husband. She left everything she had to my mother. It wasn't much. But mum loves the pendant she inherited.'

Dane froze.

'It was a pearl drop, a river pearl, we think, not valuable, but such a pretty shape. Exactly like a tear,' Persis carried on, and Dane let out his breath with sharp relief.

'Oh.'

He saw her watching him with a puzzled look and realized he was being clumsy. He managed a wry grin. 'Being a mining man, I was hoping for a tale about a nice big emerald, or even a piece of jade,' he hedged, hating himself for the deceit, even as he knew he would carry on lying. Until he had the Iris Stone back, he could do nothing else.

Persis laughed with some relief. 'Oh no. Nothing so exotic as that. Now if it had been my *grandmother's* legacy we were talking about,' she said, eyes crinkling in laughter, 'you might have been lucky. Now Angela was the kind of woman who might have had some sort of fabulous jewel given to her.'

Dane turned his head quickly to look out of the window, lest she see the sudden fury in his eyes.

'I do wish I'd known her,' Persis carried on, unaware of the danger, and looked out of the window also. At some point, half a century ago, her grandmother had probably looked out at just this landscape. And she wouldn't have found herself being bamboozled by a man. Of that Persis was sure. 'I wish she was here now.'

She would have loved Dane, of that Persis was also sure. Dane was a man's man. A real man. The kind which women of her grandmother's generation would either have appreciated or merely taken for granted.

Dane cast her a sharp, bitter glance. She was so enamoured of her grandmother, wasn't she? What would she do if he told her all about her precious Angela? That she was not just an adulteress but a gold-digging thief as well. Would she still be so quick to praise her then? And what would she do if he told her that the Canfield-Hopes, perhaps her mother, or one of her cousins, aunts or uncles, had something which belonged to him, and that he was determined to get it back, even if he had to drag them through every damned court in England?

Persis lifted her big grey eyes to his and smiled. And instantly his heart plummeted. He was going to have to hurt her, he just knew it. He could feel it.

'Dane, what's wrong?' Her sharp voice snapped him back from the edge and he blinked.

'What? Nothing. Nothing's wrong.'

Persis opened her mouth, then slowly closed it again. He hadn't seen the look on his own face. Hadn't felt the chill of foreboding which had crept into the room with them just now, like a determined, uninvited guest. But she had, and she knew it was real.

Something was standing between them.

As the train rolled on inexorably towards Alice Springs, she knew that she would have to make him tell her — whatever it was. Their happiness depended upon it. She was a woman in love, and thus was willing to give him anything and everything he wanted. But how could she when she didn't know what it was?

* * *

In her cabin that evening, Rayne Fletcher began to get ready. Tonight was the night, for better or for worse, and to hell with the world.

So what if he *was* a crook?

CHAPTER SEVEN

Alice Springs and The Ghan

Avery glanced up as the door to the restaurant car opened and let out his breath in a long, low, appreciative whistle. The group of men sitting at the table opposite heard him and quickly looked up, the two facing the wrong way craning their necks around. Avery almost laughed out loud at their expressions — he could afford to, for he knew that the blonde vision in electric blue and shimmering silver was heading for *his* table.

Rayne spotted him instantly and walked towards him, the silver tassels on the hem of her short cocktail dress swaying around her knees as she did so. Tiny spaghetti straps held the silver and blue silk creation up, displaying a vast expanse of her shoulders, neck and cleavage, which were turning golden from all the sun. Her hair, newly washed, was arranged in a curly punk-type style, which showed off the grace of her neck and the daintiness of her ears. Tiny silver and sapphire earrings were her only jewellery. She wore towering silver high heels which, combined with the sway of the train, gave her a grace in motion which she knew she'd never be able to cultivate on mere terra firma. She smiled dazzlingly at him as she approached.

Avery rose, heard the men at the next table groan in envy, grinned, and held out a chair for her. 'You should come with a government health warning,' he whispered in her ear as she sat down. 'At least half the male population in this carriage are heading for some sort of an attack.'

Rayne laughed, in just the right mood for some outrageous flattery. When a girl was going to do something stupid, it tended to help. 'In that case, let's eat quickly and go back to my place,' she purred, making him gulp ostentatiously, like a cartoon character does when faced with imminent danger.

'Yes, ma'am,' he murmured. And hastily summoned the waiter.

* * *

It was past midnight by the time they returned to her cabin though, since they'd gone on to the bar and found a deserted corridor to dance in, from music supplied by Avery's Walkman. With one earplug in his ear and, with her head resting on his shoulder, one in her own, they'd danced the night away to a combination of Procol Harum, Don McLean and The Boss. She was still ribbing him about his taste in music when she pulled open the door and walked inside, turning on the light. He slid inside and closed the door behind him and instantly the small space seemed cramped.

'Pull out the bed, would you?' she asked, watching him as he expertly did as she asked without a word. When he finished, straightened and turned towards her, she was already walking into his arms. Their lips met readily, easily, their faces just the right height for each other. She felt his hands cup her buttocks, pulling her tighter into him, and sighed noisily through her nose. With a groping hand she reached to turn off the light and a blackness that was almost total abruptly ascended. Every now and then, a light on the side of the railway line briefly lit the cabin with an eerie orange glow before plunging them into darkness once more.

In the night, they learned each other by Braille. His hands made easy work of the small hook-and-eye clasp which held her dress together at the bottom of her spine, and a snake-like slithering sound in the darkness was the only thing to mark its passing in the hot, dark void. Her fingers dealt with the small buttons of his shirt, and by the almost ticklish sensation on her fingertips, she realized that his chest was sprinkled with crisp hair. She ran her fingers through it, grabbing a few strands and tugging them just hard enough to make him wince. She laughed, then leaned forward, using her tongue as a pathfinder to first one hard button of male flesh and then the other. She felt his hand in her hair, hopelessly demolishing her hairstyle as he massaged her scalp. His harsh breathing sounded loud and incredibly erotic in the room. A single step backwards had them both tumbling onto the single bed, and she heard him chuckle, then go 'whoomph' as she landed on him, none too gently. Her fingers danced across his ribs and she felt him twitch.

'Ticklish, huh?' she whispered. 'Now that's interesting.'

'Don't you dare!'

She dropped her tongue to delve into his navel, and felt his legs jerk satisfyingly either side of her. Her hands went to his zipper and pulled down determinedly. In the darkness she felt him half sit up and firmly pushed him back. 'Uh-uh,' she muttered. She was in charge tonight. She slipped off her panties and now, totally naked, straddled him, leaning forward to cup his face in her hands. His chin was just slightly rough against hers where he needed a shave, and her fingers traced the line of his lips before kissing him again, hard.

She tugged on his trousers fretfully and he obligingly helped her by lifting his hips from the bed, long enough for her to pull them down to his ankles. Reaching up to grasp his hands in hers, she lifted his arms to above his head in a submissive gesture, and heard him grasp the sides of the mattress either side of his head. Taking him in her hand she heard him groan, a long, growling sigh which made her insides flood with liquid longing. The next moment she was guiding him into her, deep and hard, her knees gripping him either side of his thighs in compulsive reaction. She sucked in her breath, leaned back, then lifted herself, clenching him with her inner muscles all the time, then slowly repositioning herself on him again. She moved slowly, carefully, driving them both insane as she refused to listen to his hoarse pleas for her to move faster. He moved to sit up once more and yet again she firmly pushed him back, sitting down on him harder as he tried to turn her onto her side, and she heard him cry out and buck beneath her.

She hissed in her breath as her own orgasm came, went and then started to build again. He cried out her name, then, later, cried her name again.

She never did let him get on top. Not that night, anyway.

As the train rolled on to Alice Springs, that famous middle of nowhere, Rayne smiled in the darkness and tenderly kissed his exhausted body to sleep. Afterwards, she lay curled up on top of him in the narrow single bed and wondered what the hell she was going to do about him tomorrow.

* * *

Dane rose early the next morning, and wished they weren't still three days or more away from Kalgoorlie. He was sure the clue to getting the Iris Stone back lay in that dusty mining town. And if it didn't, then he'd just have to tackle the Canfield-Hope family head on. The senior member was, nominally at least, Persis's uncle, her mother's brother, so he would be the one to receive the bad news over his cornflakes. Legal action was never welcome, he'd discovered. But unless something in that damned diary of Angela's told him differently, things were about to get very bad, very fast. For all of them.

And he doubted if, at the end of it, Persis would still be looking at him with the same soft adoring eyes of the last few days. The pain at the thought of it hit him unexpectedly hard. The image of those big grey eyes turning to steel. The iron of loathing. He took a ragged breath but the constriction around his heart refused to let up, and in frustration and growing anger, he picked up the booklet on Alice Springs and began to read.

The township began, he learned, in 1871 as a repeater station on the Overland Telegraph between Adelaide and Darwin. The advent of tourism in the 1970s led to the building of comfortable hotels, sophisticated restaurants, and even a tastefully landscaped shopping mall. Gritting his teeth, he determinedly read on. If things were going to come to a head in Kalgoorlie, then he might look back on this time as the best few days of his life — the last few days he had left to freely love, and be loved in return, by Persis. He might as well make them memorable. For them both.

They'd drive up Anzac Hill, he thought, visit the obelisk memorial and get the best view of the desert and the town. The Todd River was almost certain to be dry — it rarely ever flowed — but the Charles River might be a nice setting for an evening walk. He knew Persis was looking out for something tasteful to buy her mother, whom she telephoned at most stopping places, and the Spencer and Gillen Museum, on the upper floor of the modern mall, had extensive exhibits on the art and natural history of central Australia. They were bound to have a gift shop, or give them some idea of what to look for.

But it was no good. Although, like most Australians who tended to cluster around the coastal cities, he himself had never actually been to Alice Springs before, he couldn't summon up any enthusiasm for it. Damn it, it wasn't fair.

After his too-early marriage and the almost inevitable falling apart of it, due to his many months away while touring the mines and his unsociable working hours even when in Sydney, he'd never thought much about women. Oh sure, for the occasional date. Sex. A break from the norm. The usual things. But he'd never actually thought about love. Remarriage. Children. That had all seemed light years away in the future. And, whenever he had considered it, his future wife had always been some shadowy figure — an Australian, probably, cheerful and easy-going. Someone to be comfortable with, rather than to love madly.

But now that he was madly in love, he realized how ridiculous that picture of his future had been. It had only taken a pale-faced, beautiful Englishwoman with big grey eyes and a nasty family secret to shatter that image as easily as he could shatter an empty snail shell.

But once he'd exposed Angela Canfield-Hope's big lie, and taken steps to reclaim what rightfully belonged to the Culvers and the lady in Perth . . . what then? What would be left for Persis and him then?

Dane slowly leaned forward in his chair, tossing the Alice Springs booklet aside, and let his face rest in his cupped hands. He felt bad. As bad as he'd ever felt before in his life.

And he could see no way out.

* * *

Rayne was up and dressed before Avery began to stir. Pulling open the door, she winced at the clicking sound it made. She glanced back quickly over her shoulder but he was still sound asleep. The single cotton sheet was draped half over him, giving him a rather debauched look which, she thought with a pang, really didn't go with the personality of the man at all. He was, in many ways, sweet.

She shook her head. Better not to think about last night. She'd been fey. This morning, she was an insurance investigator.

She slipped out the door and made her way to his cabin, using the key she'd found in his trouser pocket to open it up. She didn't realize that she was being watched as she slipped into his cabin. Not that she'd have needed to worry. It was no steward, up and about early and wondering what the guests were doing sneaking around at that hour, but Felix Barstow, who merely smiled and nodded to himself and went back to his own cabin.

It was about bloody time.

As he returned to his bed and curled over onto his side to get another hour or so of sleep, Rayne began to search Avery's cabin. It didn't take long. His rucksack had hardly been unpacked and nothing was in it except what she'd expected. She was wearing a pair of white cotton gloves, which she'd shoved into the pocket of her dress, and as she replaced each and every article exactly where she'd found it, she kept an ear open for the sound of approaching footsteps. What she was doing was technically illegal, and she knew it. Although her boss would throw her to the wolves if she was caught, she knew that everyone employed at her firm as investigators did things like this regularly. It was just part of the job.

The tiny and narrow wardrobe was totally empty, as were the drawers, except for a newspaper. She lifted it carefully, just going through the motions, and with no expectation at all of actually finding anything. So when she found herself looking down at a half-finished mock-up of a brochure, with the title 'Littledore Manor — Weekend and Mini-Breaks', she simply stared at it for a few unbelievably long moments. Then, reaching down and awkwardly but carefully picking it up by the corners, she lifted it out and put it on the seat of the unconverted bed. Reaching into the other pocket of her dress she withdrew a big, clear plastic bag — one of many evidence bags she always carried around with her.

She carefully slipped the brochure into the evidence bag and sealed it, all the while her face a tight, blank mask. Then she took a last look around, and left the cabin. As she headed back towards her own cabin, her mind began to function again.

OK. So here, at last, was some tangible proof that Avery was behind the scheme. Or was it? Why would he have a brochure made up at all if he planned on burning down the Manor? And why bring it to Australia?

She hesitated in the corridor, her mind racing. In fact, the more she thought about it, the more 'convenient' she found it. By the time she arrived at her own cabin again, her heart was pounding. She'd have to arrange to have the brochure flown to England straight away, and get the labs they used to check it for fingerprints. And, if Avery's weren't on it . . .

But she was getting ahead of herself. She opened the door gingerly, looked inside, saw with relief that he was still sleeping, and slipped into the room. She withdrew a plain A4 brown envelope and slipped the brochure, still safely inside the plastic covering, into it, then sealed and addressed it. Next she reached for her laptop, plugged it in, and began to compose an email to her office, warning her assistant of its imminent arrival, and her instructions regarding it. Her finger hesitated over the send button; she looked up from her seat on the floor, and with the computer still on her lap, looked at the man in her bed.

Last night had been wild. Wonderful. Quite easily the best night she'd ever had.

And she loved him.

Was she just setting herself up for a fall? She bitterly resented the old cliché of a woman making herself look like a fool because of a man, of the businesslike female coming a cropper all for the love of a rogue. She just couldn't, and wouldn't, see herself in that role. Her finger, still poised over the send button, began to waver. On the other hand, she'd always trusted her instincts. And she was good at this. She was good at what she did.

Wondering if she was making the biggest mistake of her life, she typed two more sentences.

> *Believe now that Greg Nones is a far more likely suspect than McLeod. Check him out more thoroughly — and more specifically, see if you can get a name or transfer number from the bank account listed for any future payment concerning L. Manor.*

She knew from memory that on the insurance forms, in the section where it asked for details of any payment which should be made in case of a claim, Avery McLeod's name didn't appear. Only the company name, and then the name of a specific account. Which might be an account which was available to Avery. Or then again, might not. It might be an entirely separate account which didn't even belong to Cloud Nine. If they could get the bank to co-operate (or if her PA knew a good hacker) they might just discover that the only person attached to that bank account was Greg Nones. In which case, Avery would almost certainly be in the clear.

If.

She tensed as she heard him stir, and quickly sent the email, swiftly closing the laptop. A moment later, feeling like a treacherous snake, she slipped off her dress and carefully got in beside him.

He awoke with a start, then looked at her. He needed a shave, his hair was hopelessly mussed, and he had the bleary-eyed look of anyone just waking up.

He looked gorgeous.

Rayne's heart skipped. Oh please, don't let him be a crook! 'Hello, sleepy-head,' she said. And added saucily, 'Feeling stiff?' And her knowing hand sneaked down between the covers in search of mischief, making him jump.

* * *

Felix Barstow was at the car and Jeep rental shop long before any of the other passengers from the train arrived. He had planned it that way. He checked the selection of cars on offer, feeling tense. So much of his plan depended on him being able to guess which car McLeod would choose.

The selection of cars, Jeeps and Range Rovers was large, but he'd done his research well. McLeod had a fondness for the top-of-the-range off-road vehicles, and one model, which looked brand new, a classy deep maroon in colour with all the latest on-board gadgetry, stood out from the rest. Felix looked at it from a safe distance and nodded. He waited, watching the staff inside the office carefully, and moved towards the Jeep only when the window was free of prying eyes.

He quickly lifted the hood and got to work.

* * *

Dane and Persis arrived at the car rental place at about 10.30. The train had pulled in only half an hour ago, and she'd agreed at once to a private safari with him around the 'Red Centre'. They'd gathered the makings of a picnic from one of the many shops, opting for crusty bread, soft cheese flavoured with Australian Mountain Pepperleaf, and a mixed leaf salad with loads of the native Warrigal spinach with bush tomatoes, also known as 'desert raisins'. They'd even bought a cooler for the Australian white wine Dane had selected, and a basket of fruit, including Illawarra plums.

When they got there Dane selected a big, powerful, air-conditioned sedan car, with a plush cream interior. It was one of the more expensive rentals, and Persis knew he'd chosen it with her comfort in mind. He was obviously more used to rickety Jeeps and battered mining junkers for himself, and she felt her heart swell with gratitude and pride that he was the kind of man to put her needs first.

Like a lot of Europeans, she supposed, she'd been exposed to the stereotype that Australian males were beer-swilling, misogynistic 'Sheila' haters, or plain ignorant male chauvinist pigs of the first order. Dane Culver, she knew, couldn't have been more different, despite the fact that he was an outdoors man, with a mucho-macho job and the physique of someone who could spend hours in the outback and feel at home.

She was wearing a hat, of course, because of advice from the tourist office, and had already slathered on the sun cream. Today was going to be a scorcher, she was sure. And she had only to look around at the vast expanse of red desert to know that she was in a harsh and unforgiving country.

Suddenly she was glad, very glad, that she had Dane with her.

As the car rental salesman talked with unnecessary enthusiasm about the luxury car, Persis noticed the pretty blonde English girl she'd spoken to on the train walking towards her in the company of her boyfriend. He had his arm draped casually over her shoulder, and she realized what a really wonderful-looking couple they made. And not just because they were both physically good-looking, but because, in some undeniable way, they just seemed to fit.

She glanced at Dane, and wondered, a shade whimsically and with just a touch of sadness, if they 'fit'.

And realized that she simply couldn't tell.

She smiled and the blonde woman smiled back as they passed, walked on a few yards, then stopped beside a big, tough-looking but expensive off-road vehicle in eye-catching maroon.

'Well, what do you think?' she heard the man say, and was slightly surprised by the British accent. But then, they'd probably come over together. Perhaps they were man and wife? But no, Persis somehow didn't think so.

'As if I'd ever dare challenge your taste in cars,' the blonde woman replied, grinning. 'I know what men and their cars are like. Insult this,' she pointed at the impressive Jeep, 'and you'd sulk for hours.'

The man laughed. 'Would not!'

'Would too!'

Persis grinned as she saw the English girl poke out her tongue. 'Anyway, where are we going in it? It looks fierce enough to climb a mountain,' she added, and Persis also glanced at the big tyres.

'No mountains around here,' the man replied airily. 'But I was wondering, if we drove far enough, if we might get a glimpse of Ayers Rock in the distance. It's around here somewhere.'

'It's not called Ayers Rock anymore, genius,' Rayne said, laughing, 'but by its proper native name.'

Avery rolled his eyes. 'I knew that. I was just testing. So, what do you say — shall we drive and see if we can spot it? I've got one of those collapsible telescopes that might help.'

‘Why not. We’ll need a map.’

‘I’ve got one here. See — we take this road — it’ll give us the best chance of seeing it. Mind you, with the distances involved we might only get close enough to it to make it out as a pimple on the desert’s bum, but there you are. I was wondering if we shouldn’t arrange for a two-day excursion to see it properly — you know, for the real tour, when we start offering them.’

Persis glanced away, not really eavesdropping, and not aware of how Avery’s use of the word ‘we’ had made Rayne smile then frown.

Rayne nodded. ‘Good idea,’ she said, hoping he didn’t realize how subdued she suddenly felt. For she knew, if it was proved that he was behind the insurance scam, Cloud Nine would probably fold. He’d be bankrupt, and there would be no tourists taking this particular tour down under. Or to see Uluru.

She watched as the great-looking Australian guy drove away with her fellow Brit, and sighed. She could only hope, selflessly, that the other English girl’s romance was going better than her own.

* * *

They were nearly five hours out of Alice Springs, and the road, at first easy-going, had turned into little more than a rutted track when it happened.

Rayne was enjoying herself. The rolling motion of the Jeep didn’t worry her, for it was well padded and sprung. Besides, who could complain about the state of the desert trail when the scenery was so awe-inspiring? It just never seemed to change. Moreover, it gave the impression of never being *able to change*. As if, provided they had an endless supply of petrol, she and Avery could just drive on for all eternity and never come to the end of the desert. Red sand. Scrub bush. The unforgiving hardness of the blue sky, which would have hurt her eyes but for the sunglasses. She truly felt as if she was in a place as far from home as it was possible to get. And with Avery by her side, it was an even better experience.

And then she heard it.

The sound of the engine, changing. Almost at once, she felt the Jeep begin to slow, and saw, out of the corner of her eye, Avery put his foot down harder on the accelerator. But still the Jeep slowed. Then stopped altogether. A moment later, the engine cut out, leaving them in silence.

Rayne felt her heart give a little sickening lurch.

Avery turned the ignition, gave the accelerator a pump, but nothing. He looked at her and grinned. 'Great. I wonder if AA stretch this far?'

'Don't even joke about it,' she said, grinning back. But her smile faded as he got out and lifted the hood. A minute later he was back, looking grim.

'We're not going anywhere,' he said flatly.

'Not fixable?' she asked, trying to sound upbeat.

'Not fixable,' he agreed sombrely. He didn't add that, not only was it not fixable, it looked as if it had been deliberately sabotaged. But that was absurd. He was sure the car rental place did maintenance checks regularly. It must have been a fluke. Still, he wasn't a bad mechanic, and he didn't like the looks of things under the hood.

'Oh well, we'll just have to swallow our pride and call out the cavalry,' he said, reaching for his mobile phone.

It was dead. He stared at it, weighed it in the palm of his hand. It seemed lighter than usual. Prising off the back, he realised why: the battery was missing. He glanced up and saw Rayne watching him. She too had seen the empty space, and without a word, reached into her bag for her own phone. Though she was unsure what the range was out here. But that, she realized a moment later, was a moot point anyway.

Her own battery had been removed.

Obviously, some bastard had taken the opportunity during the last twenty-four hours or so, to lift their phones and remove them. But why? And who?

'The Jeep has a CB radio, doesn't it?' she asked, trying to keep the panic from her voice.

It did.

But, surprise surprise, it wasn't working.

Avery slipped in behind the wheel and shut the door quickly. He wasn't sure how much longer the air-conditioned coolness would last without power. Soon, he was sure, the inside of the Jeep would be like a baking oven.

'We'll have to find shade soon,' he said, his voice completely calm.

Rayne caught her breath as the hideous severity of their situation suddenly hit her, and then let it out slowly. Oddly enough, she began to feel calmer. 'So we will,' she forced herself to say. 'Mind you, there's plenty to be had.' She nodded optimistically to the stunted bushes off to their right. 'Let's just hope there aren't any other critters with the same idea.'

Into her mind flashed images of poisonous snakes, funnel web spiders, black widow spiders, scorpions and all sorts in between.

'When the time comes, I'll go check it out. At least there are plenty of sticks I can poke around with.' Avery grinned. His voice, though, was strained.

Rayne nodded and glanced at her watch. 'Well, we only booked to take the car out till ten tonight. When we don't come back, they'll be sure to raise the alarm.'

'Right,' he said. Then, more cheerfully, 'Right. It's not as if we're in the age when a cow poke with a mule or a few camels was your only hope. Nowadays they'll have rescue helicopters, GPS satellites, the lot.'

Rayne nodded enthusiastically. It was silly to panic after all. 'And we've got water — plenty of it. The man in the office said we had to take gallons, if only as a precaution. Remember he sold us those two big containers in the back?'

They'd been drinking from some mineral water bottles which she'd put in her bag and in the glove compartment, but on the back seat were a couple of six-gallon containers. Enough to last them days, if necessary. Not that they'd be here days, she reminded herself firmly.

Rayne felt her skin prickle and realized she was already beginning to sweat. They wouldn't be able to stay in the Jeep for long.

'I'll refill the empty bottles from the containers,' she said. 'You go and see if anything nasty is lurking in the bushes.'

He grinned, admiring her more in that moment than he'd ever admired her before. Oh, he'd wanted her before, and loved her, and been charmed by her. Now, her bravery only added itself to the list of all the things he liked about her. Any other woman, he was sure, would have been having hysterics on him by now. But not his Rayne.

'Deal,' he said cheerfully.

Perhaps it was her training kicking in, or sheer luck, or maybe even divine guidance. She was never to know what made her check the containers before she poured them into the bottles. But if she hadn't done so, she might have poured the water from the gallon containers into the only half-bottle of good water they had left.

As it was, she found herself pouring some water from the container into her cupped hand before she was even aware of giving herself the command to do so. And when she lifted her hand to her mouth, she knew it wasn't the result of her own sweat which made the water taste so appallingly salty.

Quickly, she spat it out, feeling sick. As she did so, Avery came around the back of the Jeep and stared at her. 'What are you doing?' he asked sharply. We can't afford to waste it!'

Slowly, her face totally blank, Rayne screwed the top back on the big plastic container then looked at him.

'We can't afford to drink it, either,' she said, her voice sounding strange and far off.

She saw him go pale. 'What do you mean?' he asked stiffly.

'It's tainted,' she said flatly, and reached up to wipe a trickle of perspiration which was rolling down her forehead. The air was arid and fierce with heat. Their eyes met, and then dropped to the single half-bottle of water she was holding.

'We're in trouble, aren't we?' Rayne finally said quietly.

And slowly, reluctantly, Avery nodded.

CHAPTER EIGHT

Alice Springs and The Ghan

Persis walked to her wardrobe and glanced inside. She had been very careful when she'd packed her cases back in England, always mindful of the fact that as her itinerary called for a lot of packing and unpacking, not to mention baggage handling nearly every day, she couldn't afford to be over-indulgent. So she'd been very strong-minded and confined herself to thin sundresses which took up little room, only two extra pairs of shoes, and a modest toiletries bag. She'd also packed only one smart jacket which went well with several different shades of skirt and blouse, and, overall, had been very pleased with her self-restraint.

But on the eve of her departure she'd succumbed, and added her favourite gown. She wasn't sure why — she'd never really expected to wear it. Perhaps it had been a safety blanket for her — a kind of mental safety net, something familiar and luxurious which she could take with her. So far it had lain, folded and forgotten, in the zipper part of the lid, safe and secure. Now it hung on a hanger, ironed and free of even the mildest of creases.

For a long moment, she looked at it thoughtfully. Was it too much? Or was tonight *really* the night to wear it? Certainly, Dane was taking her out to dine in style, in one of the Alice's most prestigious restaurants, and he'd hinted at dancing afterwards. But more than that, it felt *psychologically* right. They were lovers now — albeit precarious ones. He'd seen her naked. Now she felt in need of just a little feminine armour. To engineer a shot-across-his-bows moment which told him in no uncertain terms that he'd still better stay on his toes.

She nodded in decision, glanced at the clock on the wall and went to the shower. She shampooed and double-conditioned her hair, blow-drying it into flowing, gloriously glossy and very dark brown waves, which tumbled around her pale face and about her neck and ears to reach just past her shoulders. Reaching for two dark tortoiseshell clips, which all but disappeared in her hair, she positioned them so that they swept back her tresses, as if by magic, to expose her ears and the sides of her neck. She reached for her limited selection of jewellery and added her favourite pair of earrings — two delicate pear-drops of amber in a lacy, silver filigree setting. They dangled just far enough to cast a delightful shadow over her shoulders and when she moved her head she could feel them lightly touch the sides of her neck as they swung.

Her make-up she kept simple, her fine pale skin needing little in toner or powder. She added a peachy-red lipstick and a mere smearing of silvery eyeshadow, which did marvellous things for her grey eyes. Next she slipped on a full-length silk underskirt and a pair of silvery-grey shoes. She'd have preferred them to be a bit more ritzy and with a higher heel, but she'd chosen them to be both sensible and passable for evening wear, and when she fastened the buckles around her ankles, was pleased to note that the sheer silk tights she was wearing elevated the shoes to new heights.

Satisfied, she walked to the wardrobe and brought out the dress, stroking the gossamer-fine silk lovingly. The dress had been a major extravagance last summer, and she'd only worn it twice before. Now she slipped it over her head, hoping she hadn't lost too much weight to make it look ridiculous.

She hadn't.

In the mirror she glanced back at her reflection and turned this way and that, smoothing the dress over her hips, waist and stomach. It had the look of raw silk and was of a perfectly clear apricot shade. In different lights the silk seemed to glow with shifting colours as she moved, from milky white to deeper orange. With her dark hair and silver accessories, she looked wonderful, and she knew it.

All right, Dane. Better batten down the hatches!

* * *

In the desert, night had fallen cold and hard. From sweating and cursing, Avery and Rayne had gone to shivering and cursing. The water bottle held only a few mouthfuls each; despite their determination to be strong and save at least half of their water for tomorrow, they'd been unable to keep to that promise. Dehydration had set in with alarming swiftness, and although they'd set up a makeshift cover from a plastic sheet they'd found in the back of the Jeep, thus saving them from the worst effects of heatstroke, things had got very bad very quickly.

First Rayne then Avery had begun to feel dizzy, and their voices had become hoarse the longer they'd struggled to go without a drink. The at first merely appalling but then utterly insatiable desire to drink had plagued them for hours, forcing them to keep taking tiny sips at their precious supply of water. When the sun had begun to set, Rayne had rejoiced. Surely, now that the fierce sun wasn't so intent on desiccating them like two human coconuts, they could leave off the water?

But she hadn't counted on the cold. Or the sensation of utter desolation.

They were laid out on the desert floor, curled like a pair of spoons against one another for maximum body heat and mutual comfort. She wanted to sob like a baby on his shoulder, but she'd be damned if she would. But she couldn't think of anything upbeat to say either. At first they'd joked away the hours, trying to pretend that everything would be all right. That their predicament was merely inconvenient; uncomfortable, a little worrying, perhaps, but definitely survivable. But, along with the water and the strength of their voices, she knew that their hope was fading as well. And she could do nothing to hold onto it.

She shook her head and nuzzled closer and felt his arm tighten around her. Unbelievably, she slept.

* * *

Dane Culver glanced up from the magazine he was pretending to read. He was in the small lobby of the hotel, and already she was ten minutes late. He didn't understand why she'd asked to meet him down here in the first place — their rooms, after all, were more or less adjoining. Then he looked up as a movement on the curved staircase opposite alerted him, and he suddenly didn't care why. Or that she was late. Or that he was in a hopeless jam.

She was a vision.

It was fully dark outside, and the hotel lobby's orange-tinted lights only added to the effect of her stood there like some pagan queen, one hand holding lightly onto the banister, her dark locks as impressive as any crown. Her left leg was slightly forward of the other and bent at the knee, making the silk evening gown she wore swirl back and cling to the calf of her other leg. The deep V-neck exposed the sides of her breasts, enough to make his heart pound, while still almost primly within the bounds of good taste.

He stood up slowly, unaware that his face was a mask of granite. From across the lobby, and from her spot looking down on him, Persis had no idea what he was thinking. She watched him as he walked up to her and came to rest at the bottom of the stairs, looking up into her face. His dark green eyes gleamed like jade.

'You look . . . incredible,' he said finally. And without any pretence at flattery. So it was, of course, the most flattering thing she'd ever heard in her life. Or probably ever would.

She smiled radiantly. 'Thank you.'

He was dressed in bottle-green slacks and a cream-coloured shirt. He was tie-less, but somehow managed to give the ensemble the look of a man dressed in a best tux. Her heart flipped then sailed as he held out his hand. Wordlessly she walked down the few remaining steps and took it.

* * *

'What time is it?' Rayne asked, and, in the utter darkness of the desert, felt Avery twist and check his watch.

'Dunno. The damned thing's supposed to be luminous, but I can't make it out. I don't think it can be too late though. Perhaps midnight?'

Rayne nodded and wearily dropped her head back onto her forearm. Apart from the catnap which she'd just had, she knew she wasn't going to sleep again that night. She wondered, instead, if she was going to die. Seriously. It was a strange thing to think about. She didn't like it, and thought of something else.

'Avery.'

'What?'

'Make love to me.'

For a second he was utterly still, then he rolled over so that he was facing her. In the dark she could barely make out the shape of his face. She heard, rather than saw, him reach out, and a moment later his finger was tracing the line of her cheek. She nuzzled her face into his cupped palm, like a cat begging to be stroked, and heard him sigh.

'Tomorrow,' he said softly. 'When we're back in town, and there's a nice comfy double bed to be had.'

Rayne laughed. How had he known the right thing to say?

'Deal,' she said softly. And then turned her face away quickly, in case he should feel the tears which were forcing their way past her eyes and rolling down her cheeks.

* * *

Persis enjoyed their midnight stroll along the river. The water, though very low, nevertheless reflected the moonlight, and away in the darkness, strange animals gave eerie calls. It was cold, much colder than she'd expected, but Dane, who'd had his jacket in the car, had long since draped it across her shoulders. Now they emerged back onto the tarmac of the road and glanced across at the neon lights.

'More dancing?' he asked, but she shook her head.

'No. Let's go back to the hotel,' she said softly. And hoped he understood what she was saying. She thought he did, for his hand reached out to hers and clasped her fingers in a wordless, almost heartbreakingly tender grip, which was, nevertheless, eloquent with desire.

When they reached the lobby, however, they both instantly sensed that something was wrong. The desk clerk was talking anxiously to a man dressed in what was obviously a policeman's uniform. Their voices dropped as the door opened, and they both turned to look at the new arrivals with rather more than a passing interest.

Persis saw the clerk shake his head to something the policeman said. Dane, too, was watching them, his eyes narrowing. 'Wait here a minute,' he said abruptly, and walked towards the desk.

Persis lingered by the stairs and watched, a feeling of foreboding stealing over her as Dane listened, glanced her way, listened some more, shrugged and turned away. When he got closer to her, she lifted her eyebrow in query. 'What's wrong?'

'Two guests haven't returned, apparently. They checked in here this morning, saying they were going to rent a car and explore. Apparently the car rental people informed the police when they were overdue, as they're obliged to, and Officer Stevens over there is trying to check up on them. But they've not returned here either. I told them we'd been out on the town but hadn't seen them. Not that that means anything — the Alice isn't exactly a one-horse town anymore.'

Persis listened and began to frown. 'Who are they?'

'An Avery McLeod and one Rayne Fletcher.'

The names meant nothing to Persis. 'What do they look like? Are they Australian?'

'No — both poms.' He stopped abruptly as Persis reached out and grabbed his arm, her grip surprisingly hard. She'd gone pale. Persis couldn't have said why, but she was suddenly utterly sure she knew who he was talking about. 'Is she a small blonde, pert and pretty? And is he a few inches shorter than you with dark hair?'

Dane looked at her sharply, and nodded. 'That's the description Officer Stevens gave me. Why? Do you know them?'

'Yes. No. I mean, I spoke to her once on the train. And I noticed them again this morning. They were hiring their car the same time as us. You probably didn't see — you were negotiating for the car.'

Dane took her arm gently and began to lead her back to the desk. 'I think you'd better talk to Stevens,' he said softly, keeping his voice calm and soothing. As a native, he knew how unforgiving the outback could be, but he didn't want to frighten her.

The policeman, hearing his name being mentioned, turned from the desk, looking at them curiously as they approached. Briefly, Dane explained, then Stevens turned to Persis. He was one of those weather-beaten men with crinkly grey hair and skin like tanned leather, who could have been any age from fifty to eighty.

'I don't suppose you heard them say where they were headed, young lady?' he asked, in a broad Australian accent.

'Yes. I heard the man say he wanted to see if he could see Ayers Rock. Even in the distance.'

The policeman glanced at the clerk, who raised his eyebrows but said nothing. Persis had the idea that lost tourists wasn't anything new to him, but nevertheless, she was sure she caught a gleam of real concern in his eyes as he turned away to fiddle with the switchboard.

'Is that so. Did he say which route he was going to take by any chance?' Officer Stevens persisted, but already Persis was shaking her head.

'I'm afraid not.'

The policeman nodded. 'Well, fair enough. At least now we know which direction to look. And he picked for himself a pretty sturdy vehicle. Knowing young fellas like I do, I bet he couldn't resist trying it out on one of the wilder roads. I reckon he'll be up somewhere around Kingaroona Wilds. Well, that'll give the pilot a place to start.'

'They will be all right, won't they?' Persis asked anxiously. In her mind's eye, she could see the pretty blonde woman again, smiling at her as she walked past, looking as if she didn't have a care in the world.

'Sure to be — no worries,' the officer said. 'The fella at the car rental sold them two six-gallon water drums. Even if we don't find 'em tomorrow, they'll still be fine the next day. They might be a bit hot and bothered, but they've got the Jeep, which means they've also got shade and protection. And water's the main thing. They'll be fine.'

He sounded indulgent and not a little annoyed at poms who had no bush sense, but he didn't sound worried.

Much relieved, Persis turned back to Dane, who smiled at her gently. 'Your place or mine?' he asked softly.

Persis smiled. 'You choose,' she said. And let him lead her up the stairs.

* * *

In the desert, Rayne told herself that she wasn't really thirsty. She just thought she was. It was too cold to be really thirsty.

She half-dozed, dreaming of icicles. Icicles which melted in her mouth, flooding her parched throat with cool water.

She started into full consciousness, knowing that soon it would be light again. And hot again. And they had only a few mouthfuls of water left. Why hadn't either she or Avery told anyone where they were going? No doubt at first light the rescue planes would be out — but they had no idea where to look for them. It was an enormous amount of ground to cover; it could take them days to find them. And she knew they didn't have days.

Just how long did it take the average human to die of thirst? She had no idea. She thought, perhaps, that that was just as well. Then she felt Avery's hand slip into hers, warming her numbed fingers, and she sighed.

'I love you,' Avery whispered in the dark.

'I love you too,' Rayne whispered back.

* * *

Rayne woke the next morning, surprised to realize she'd actually been asleep. She sat up, feeling stiff and sore after her night on the desert floor.

And thirsty.

Beside her, Avery scrambled to his feet, winced and stretched. 'Well, another lovely day in the outback,' he said, his voice as dry as the desert air. He coughed, then wished he hadn't. He glanced at the water bottle then quickly away again. Neither of them dared drink.

'What do you suppose our fellow guests are having back at Alice right now?' she said instead, making him groan.

'Shut up, woman. If I'd known you had these masochistic tendencies, I'd never have—'

'Shut up!' she snapped, leaping to her feet, making him pause mid-word, his mouth slightly open as he gaped at her.

'What?'

But then he heard it too. An unmistakable sound.

'Helicopter!' Rayne said, unnecessarily. Then, 'Quick, let's get out from under cover. They might not see us!' Her voice had risen in panic, and Avery grabbed her as she ran past.

'Relax. They might miss us, but they're not likely to miss the Jeep.' Nevertheless, he ran to the Jeep, fiddled with something on the side of it, then looked up into the sky. So far, neither of them could spot the sound where the faint noise was coming from — there wasn't even a dot in the clear blue sky as a pointer.

Then she saw that he was angling the wing mirror, making it catch the sun, flashing out a silent SOS to anyone watching from the skies.

She slowly leaned against the Jeep, the metal of which was already uncomfortably hot from the sun, and began to pray.

Let them see us.

Please let them see us.

'There it is!' Avery cried, still angling the mirror but pointing excitedly with his other hand. And now Rayne could see it too. A dark red dot, getting larger.

'And it's not even eight o'clock yet,' she said admiringly, glancing at her watch. 'Now that's what I *call* a rescue service. We'll even be back in time, I bet, to catch the two o'clock train out of here.'

Avery, still anxiously watching the approaching helicopter and carefully aiming his flashing mirror more or less, he hoped, right in the pilot's eyes, found himself grinning like a loon. 'What? Not anxious to stay around?'

Rayne laughed giddily. 'Just call me a killjoy.'

The helicopter was now, without a doubt, making straight for them. 'You beauty,' Avery said appreciatively.

'Thank you, kind sir,' Rayne said, silly with relief.

'Oh yeah. You too,' Avery said, deadpan.

* * *

Felix Barstow watched the police car pull into the parking lot of the hotel and ground his teeth as he saw the blonde insurance investigator and Avery McLeod climb from the back of it. They looked weary, dusty, but disgustingly cheerful.

Without a word, he turned on his heel and headed for the nearest bar. It should have worked. Fixing the car to break down after a good few hours, thus ensuring they were far into the outback, had been easy. As had destroying the CB radio. Spiking the water had been harder, but he'd been lucky there. He'd saved up a good supply of salt by simply pocketing the little sachets found in restaurants and on the train. He'd guessed that the two containers which the car rental clerk had retrieved and left in the small office had been bound for his latest customers, and had made quick work of slipping in the salt. He'd even stayed to watch Avery himself collect the tainted water and take it to the truck. What's more, he'd then waited around a while longer, getting into casual conversation with another member of the staff and managing to find out that nobody there knew exactly where the young English couple had been heading for.

But he was aware of Avery's reputation as a bit of an explorer, the kind who liked to push the boundaries of a holiday experience, and had guessed that he wouldn't be able to resist an impromptu trip into the outback. So how had the rescue services found them so quickly?

Damn.

Damn, damn, damn.

He ordered himself a big Scotch and sighed heavily. Now it was back to that bloody train again.

And plan C.

* * *

As Felix drowned his sorrows in Scotch, Officer Stevens was giving Avery and Rayne a lecture on life in the bush. He also told them that they probably owed if not their lives then at least their early rescue to fellow tourists, who'd just happened to overhear their plans.

By mutual and unspoken consent, they let him talk himself out, then Rayne glanced at Avery, who nodded.

'I think you'd better have a mechanic check out our Jeep, Officer,' Rayne said, the sombreness of her voice making him stiffen.

'And our water,' Avery put in.

'And the radio,' Rayne added.

'And our mobile phones,' Avery continued, while the policeman looked from one to the other, like a man at a tennis match. 'He must have raided our cabins at some point. He was a very resourceful man!'

Ten minutes later he left, looking exceedingly grim.

In Avery's room, where they'd congregated for the showdown, Rayne slowly flopped back on the bed where she'd been sitting, and sighed. The helicopter's co-pilot had given them a bottle of water each on landing, followed by general sympathy. The flight back to the town, though, had been nothing less than awe-inspiring. Perhaps because they'd been given their lives back, or perhaps because it was Rayne's first flight in a whirly-bird, the hours in the air had seemed especially magical.

From the sky, the vastness of the desert had rendered them speechless and humble. To think they'd been lost in all of that, and then been found. Now, of course, things could never be the same. She opened her eyes and looked up at him as he stood, looking down at her. She raised her hand and wriggled her fingers invitingly at him. He raised one eyebrow, making no move to take them.

She grinned. 'Remember what you promised me last night? About when we were back in town and the services of a nice double bed were on offer? Well,' she said, and patted the mattress invitingly beneath her.

'Oh. That,' he said, and slowly stretched out over her. 'Do I get to be on top this time?' Rayne reached up and hooked her legs behind his bum. 'If you're good.'

He laughed at that and shook his head. 'You're outrageous,' he said softly, and kissed her hard. When he lifted his head she was feverishly unbuttoning his shirt. He wondered if he should tell her that he'd also meant the other thing he'd told her last night. About loving her. But somehow — he gasped as she bit his shoulder with a demanding, feverish need — now didn't seem the right time.

They made love as only two people who'd faced the imminent prospect of death *could* make love; with a lust for life and for each other which swept over them, tossed them about like a cork on a lazy ocean, and finally left them stranded on the shore, satiated, sweating, gasping and grateful.

* * *

The Ghan left Alice Springs at two that afternoon, and in spite of Officer Steven's objections, both Rayne and Avery were on it. At the station he just had time to confirm that the Jeep *had* been sabotaged, as had the radio, and that common salt was probably the main contaminant in the canisters of water. His men, he'd told them, were even now making enquiries at both the car rental place and in town. He promised to keep in touch with them after demanding, and receiving from Avery, a full list of their itinerary and where they could be reached. With new batteries installed in their phones, he made sure he took down their numbers.

But as the train pulled away, and Avery watched from the door window as the figure of Officer Stevens got smaller and smaller, he wasn't at all sure that they were doing the right thing in leaving so soon.

But Rayne really hadn't been kidding when she'd said she didn't want to stay in Alice Springs a moment longer than necessary, and he could understand why.

As the train headed for Heavitree Gap, and the long haul back to Tarcoola, he too felt a sense of relief to leave the place behind.

Someone had tried to kill them.

It was fantastic. Unbelievable. The more he thought about it, the more he thought it must be a mistake of some kind. A case of mistaken identity perhaps. Or maybe the assassin had picked the wrong Jeep. He might even have picked up the water which had been meant for someone else. After all, there were thousands of tourists in Alice Springs.

It must be a mistake. He knew of nobody who wanted to kill him. But . . . what about Rayne? He tensed as the hot air swept over his face and the dust of Alice Springs was left behind. What did he really know about Rayne? She worked as a secretary. *She said.* Her family, from what little she'd told him, all sounded perfectly normal and above board. *From what she'd told him.*

But it was just as ridiculous to think that someone was after *her* as it was to think that somebody wanted *him* dead.

As he made his way back to his cabin, he didn't see Felix Barstow cast at his back an expression of frustrated loathing. Avery didn't know it, but he hadn't left danger behind in Alice Springs after all. It had merely followed him onto the train.

But he would find that out. And soon.

CHAPTER NINE

Tarcoola and the Indian Pacific

The next day, they arrived back in Tarcoola at a little after 2 p.m. Nearly all the passengers who would later be catching the *Indian Pacific* on its way to Perth had opted to rent a hotel room for the day and half the night, as the train boarded at a yawn-making 4.28 a.m. the following morning.

Avery booked a double room at the best hotel in town and wondered if he should tackle Rayne about any possible enemies she hadn't told him about. He wasn't looking forward to it. I mean, just how did you ask the woman you loved if there was somebody out there who wanted her dead?

'By the way, babe, you're not the ex-wife of a villain or some psychotic husband, are you?' Or how about, *'Hey, Rayne, you didn't steal some money from the London branch of whoever took over from the Kray Twins, did you?'* Or even, *'I don't suppose you're some undercover cop secretly on the run from a bad guy who's put out a contract on you, are you?'*

He didn't bother to unpack, but watched her covertly as she slung her own case, rather wearily, next to the wardrobe and moved to the window to look out. Was it his imagination, or was she a woman with something heavy on her mind?

'You want first dibs on the bathroom?' he asked gallantly, and she surprised him somewhat by shaking her head.

'Nah, you go ahead.'

He nodded, realizing it was no good tackling her until he had some sort of coherent plan in mind — he'd probably only succeed in putting her back up.

Rayne watched him go into the bathroom and, immediately as he shut the door behind him, headed briskly for the door and out into the corridor. Downstairs, in the lobby, she quickly phoned home. She knew it was practically the middle of the night back in England and expected to merely leave a message on the answerphone in her office, but she was in for a surprise. Her PA wasn't there, but her secretary Mona Dickinson, a somewhat dizzy married woman with four children, was. She answered it on the second ring.

'Oh, Miss Fletcher. How are things going? I bet it's nice and warm down there, even though it's their winter. It's raining here.'

Rayne smiled at her typically breathless greeting, and asked what she was doing still at work.

'Oh, there's some flap on,' Mona said vaguely. 'Mr Cole asked me if I could come in and get some papers ready. They have to arrive in Amsterdam first thing.'

Rayne hoped that one of their diamond merchant clientele hadn't been robbed, but since she had other things on her mind right now, asked crisply if her PA had left any messages for her.

'Uh-huh. I have them here. Just a moment, Miss Fletcher.' Rayne heard some rustling over the wire, then a slight cough as Mona put on her best dictation voice. 'The brochure you had sent over special delivery was totally devoid of fingerprints.'

'Yes!' Rayne cried, holding her fist in the air and then yanking it down in a telling, triumphant gesture. There was a startled pause on the other end of the line, then a stifled giggle.

'Er, I take it that's good news, Miss Fletcher. There's another message about handwriting. Do you want to hear it?'

Rayne fought back the urge to snap that of course she wanted to hear it, and merely said a rather meek, 'Yes please,' instead.

Again her secretary cleared her throat. 'It is the opinion of two separate experts that the samples of the handwritten specimens this office gave them, of the signature of a Mr Avery McLeod, do not match. Although it was the opinion of one of them that it was the work of an expert, rather than an amateur forger, both agreed that the same man did not write the two samples.'

Rayne, grinning from ear to ear, thanked Mona and was about to hang up, then had second thoughts. 'Oh, is Mr Cole actually in the office?'

'Yes. But I'm not sure if he's busy. He's been on the phone all night. Shall I ask his secretary if he's available?' Mona, who went in awe of anyone bearing the same name as one of the company's three partners, didn't sound very eager to tackle one of their august secretaries either.

'No, just put me straight through to his office.'

'Oh, but, Miss Fletcher—'

'Please, Mona,' Rayne interrupted firmly, in her very effective, no-nonsense voice. There was a beep and a purr as the phone system did an internal hiccough, and then she heard her boss's voice.

'Yes? Who is it?'

'It's me, Matt. Rayne. It's very late over there, or should I say early,' she said, but her tone of voice indicated she didn't really want to know, and no doubt Cole wouldn't be eager to talk about a crisis over the phone anyway.

'It's more or less sorted,' he said gruffly, confirming her suspicions. 'So, what's up? I've been following your requests from down under. Am I wrong, or is it beginning to look as if we've got the wrong partner under scrutiny?'

'I'd say so,' she said. Since he'd been kept informed about the lack of fingerprints and the forged signature, she didn't mention them, but launched straight into an account of what had happened at Alice Springs. Her boss, a tough but not insensitive man — who, far into middle age, had three daughters Rayne's own age — listened in an ominous silence.

'You think it was a deliberate attempt on your life?' he said when she was finished, the concern and anger evident, even over the telephone line.

'Well, the Jeep was definitely tampered with, and there was no way that I could see how salt could have been accidentally introduced to the car rental's supply of water. But I don't think it was me they were after,' she added, after a pause. And her boss, a wily insurance man of over two decades standing, was there in a flash.

'If the target was McLeod, we've got to be looking at Greg Nones then. You know, he's been doing some mighty interesting business with his bank recently. If I were the suspicious kind, I might just think he was getting ready to rabbit.'

Thousands of miles away, Rayne nodded happily. 'Yes. And probably with the company funds too. Have you given Cloud Nine any indication of when we might pay up for the fire at Littledore?'

'No,' Matt Cole said grimly. 'So he might have given up on it. And if you're right about what happened in Alice Springs, he might have hired someone to foul things up. With McLeod dead or missing, it'll be twice as hard to bring any account of wrongdoing back to our Mr Nones's door. Any defence lawyer would simply point to the missing or dead partner and point out that McLeod had as much opportunity for fraud as Nones.'

'Right. So what do we do?'

'Oh, I've already got Nones under tight surveillance. Now I think it's time to call in the police. If he does rabbit, we'll need their help, not to mention the airport and ports authority people. You'd better give me the name of the investigating officer down there, so I can clue him in. It might help. What was it again?'

'Stevens. So . . .' Rayne took a deep breath and crossed her fingers. 'Do you want me to come home? Or should I keep tabs on McLeod?'

There was a brief silence, then Matt Cole sighed. 'No, you'd better stay on him. We'll handle things this end.'

'OK,' Rayne said, trying not to let her jubilation show. 'I'll give you a progress report when we get to Kalgoorlie.' After a few more words, Rayne hung up, and all but hugging herself with glee, trotted back to their room. It didn't hurt her promotion chances any for the boss to know that she could handle physical danger and pressure as well as the more mental stresses which came with the job. She could almost see her name plate on her brand-new desk in her bigger office right now. Another four years, six max, and she'd be a partner.

Damn straight she would!

Avery, wearing nothing but water droplets and a small white towel wrapped around his waist, looked up with an anxious frown as she threw open the door and marched in. 'There you are. I thought you'd deserted me.'

'No way, Jose,' she said, eyeing him hungrily. And gave a huge grin. 'I'm so glad you're not a crook.'

'What?' he asked, startled, but then she was on him. From a running start she all but threw herself into his arms. He caught her deftly but staggered back, the bed hitting him behind the knees and making him fold over backwards. She landed on top of him as he bounced, kissing him hungrily, her mouth hot and intent, her tongue a foraging invader seeking enemy tonsils. He felt his loins harden instantly and managed to drag in a noisy breath through his nose. She lifted her head, but only so she could nibble his throat, his ear lobes and the cords in his neck, and explore the valleys and hills of his shoulders.

He tasted of shower water and man. His hands moved under her blouse, fanning out across her back and undoing her bra. Impatiently, she shucked off her clothes, too needy to bother with a slow and leisurely striptease. She could do that tomorrow, on the train.

He barely had time to rise onto his elbows before she was back again, as naked as himself. She whipped off the towel and dipped her head, tracing the muscles of his thighs, slowly licking her way until she was sucking on first one then the other ball of silken flesh. She felt his skin tighten and heard him gasp as his back arched off the bed. She lifted her head, loving the way she'd painted a hot flush of desire high across his cheekbones, then yelped as he suddenly rolled her onto her side. Coming up behind her, he lifted her leg and slid smoothly into her, making her gasp and throw her head back, to lie across one of his shoulders. His hand came around to cup one breast, which he kneaded erotically in time to his thrusts.

Rayne swallowed hard then breathed even harder as she felt her climax build. She stiffened, unable to move, as he continued to push her ruthlessly and wonderfully to the edge. Then he started all over again.

It was going to be a long, lovely afternoon.

* * *

Dane Culver didn't know it, but the phone he picked up was still warm from Rayne's telephone conversation, as he selected the same phone in the lobby barely a minute after she'd finished using it. He dialled, from memory, the telephone number of the hospital in Perth.

'Oh yes, Mr Culver. She's awake. I'll take the phone through to her now.' The ward sister, recognizing his voice, wasted little time in connecting them. Dane waited, and a moment later came a familiar voice. It was weak now with the stroke which had first decimated her less than a month ago, but still held all the warmth and love he remembered.

'Dane. Is that you?'

'Yes, Gran,' he said hoarsely. 'How are you doing?'

'You know how I'm doing. I'll be glad to see you again. Do you have it yet?'

Dane hated to say it, but knew he had to. 'No. But by the time I get to Perth and can come in and see you, I'll either know where it is, who has it, or how I can get it — likely all three. I promise,' he reiterated.

'I know you will. I have faith in you. I always have.'

Dane swallowed back the emotion which clogged his throat. It was true — his grandmother had always believed in him. So much so that she'd voted for him to take over as chairman of Culver Enterprises when his father had died, when he was only twenty-two and fresh from university. Other members of the board had all been for appointing an interim chairman, a man of known experience. But Dane had wanted the job and had pitched for it. Although he'd inherited all his father's shares and his mother, obviously, voted his way, it still wouldn't have been enough to get him the job, had his grandmother not voted his way also. And he'd repaid her trust in him a hundred times over since. Culver Enterprises was now one of the biggest producers of opals anywhere in the world. And he'd doubled their holdings in metal in Broken Hill. He was also showing Kalgoorlie's biggest mine operators that there was another kid on the block too. But none of that mattered now.

His grandmother was dying.

And she wanted the Iris Stone back. To be able to hold it and bathe in the beauty of its light one more time before she died. And Dane would see to it that it happened.

'I'll be in Perth on Saturday,' he said softly. 'I love you, Gran.' *Don't die.* He closed his eyes painfully. *Wait for me.*

As if able to read his mind, the redoubtable old lady in Perth laughed softly into the phone. 'I'll still be here, Dane, don't worry.'

Dane nodded, believing her, said his goodbyes softly, and hung up. He'd never known his grandfather, Walter — only his wife, Jennifer, the woman whose voice still echoed now in his mind. It was from Jennifer that he'd learned, as a boy, how his grandmother and grandfather had met, at a society dance in Sydney. About how her family, a conservative newspaper dynasty, hadn't taken to the rough and, at the time, penniless prospector. He'd listened, fascinated, as she'd told him how they'd eloped, and how her family had disowned her. As a ten-year-old boy, he'd been fascinated, time and time again, by the story of how Walter had found gold, that most miraculous and glamorous of metals, not two years after they were married. But not a fortune in gold. No real-life fairy tale was ever that simple or that emphatic.

So his grandmother, at Dane's bidding, had related time and time again how years of poverty and hardship had followed as Walter had doggedly worked his claim, and how they'd celebrated when his own mother had been born. And then, Jennifer would say, smiling down at her rapt grandson's face, one day, an old friend of Walter's had lain dying, and for the price of a trip back to town and the services of a doctor, her husband had bought what both Walter and the original owner had thought to be a useless mine. Until, two days after his friend had died, Walter had found opals.

And not just any opals. Fine-quality gem opals. And, what's more, a year and a day after buying the mine, he found 'it'.

It was always at this point in the tale that the young Dane had become too excited to sit still, and his grandmother had always admonished him and told him she wouldn't finish the story unless he did so. It had been near quitting time, she'd explained, her voice dreamy with remembrance. The sun was setting, and she, Walter's wife, was waiting for him back home with supper. By now they'd managed to build for themselves a proper house, the old caravan in which they'd previously lived being let out to one of the miners. Walter's men had all quit for the day, but *something* had told Walter to have just one more go with the pick, just one more time. And it was this which had always stirred the young Dane's imagination. It had been like magic.

He could almost picture it — his grandfather, covered in dirt and grime and sweat at the end of the day, deep in the bowels of the earth with only his lamp for lighting, suddenly getting some other-worldly message to take one more swing with the pick.

And Walter had done so. And there it was. Milky white, gleaming with all the colours of the rainbow. 'The Iris Stone,'

Dane would breathe reverently, his child's face lit up as he imagined his long-dead grandfather finding Australia's most famous stone.

'The Iris Stone,' his grandmother would echo, a wealth of pride and humility in her voice as she breathed the wondrous name. 'The Iris Stone. Which he set in an oval of gold and put on a chain. Just for me.'

But then Dane would ask why he couldn't see it, and it always made his grandmother cry. He quickly learned not to ask for it again. And it wasn't until his mother thought that he was old enough to understand that he was ever told what had really happened to the Iris Stone.

Namely, that his grandfather had given it away to his mistress. An English temptress and gold-digger called Angela Canfield-Hope.

Now, as he hung up the phone and walked slowly back to the room where Angela's granddaughter awaited him, he felt as if he had the weight of the world upon his shoulders. He was hopelessly torn between the woman who'd stood by him and loved him all his life, and the woman he loved and hoped to spend the rest of his life with from now on.

He knew how much he owed to the past, and the woman who now lay slowly dying in Perth, and Dane would do everything in his power to fulfil her dying wish. But what did he owe to the woman he loved? The woman who was his future?

When old Walter C (as Angela referred to him in her damned diaries) had first found the stone, it had made headline news in all the newspapers. Firstly, because it was the biggest opal ever found in Australia. Secondly, because it was discovered by a dirt-poor, independent miner, who'd found it with his own bare hands and a pick — and this alone made it the stuff of legends. But mostly it was its unusual beauty and the fantastic way that nature and sheer chance had shaped the colours within it that had rendered the Iris Stone so gloriously fabulous. His grandmother had been the most envied woman in Australia whenever she wore it. Which, between the wars, wasn't often, as glamorous occasions were few and far between.

Then Walter had died, and his wife had been quick to say that she would never wear the stone in public again. Too humiliated to tell the world that her husband had given it away to a lover, she preferred to maintain the legend of the Iris Stone being locked away in a vault, too painful a reminder of the man she loved for its mistress to ever wear it again.

But now she was dying, and with her death, she feared the truth about it would come to light. After all, Dane's own mother would be expected to give the stone a much-anticipated wearing — after a decent interval, of course. And so his grandmother had asked him to get the stone back. With the phenomenal success he'd made of Culver Enterprises, he knew he could afford to simply *buy* it back, since he hardly expected the Canfield-Hopes to do the decent and morally correct thing and just *hand* it over.

But however he retrieved it, he needed to do it *discreetly*, if at all possible. And by legal force if all else failed. No matter how acrimonious it became. And now, upstairs, Persis Canfield-Hope waited for him. Believing herself to be loved. As she was. But would she believe it when she found out the truth? After all, *he* could hardly believe it himself. If someone had told him only last month that he'd fall head over heels in love with a Canfield-Hope, he'd have laughed himself sick.

But he *was* in love with her. And he *did* believe her to be innocent of any knowledge of her grandmother's perfidy. Any doubts he'd once had that she was as culpable as her damned grandmother had long since died a good-riddance death. But what good would his faith in her do him now? What good would it do either of them? Because, before they got to Perth, he'd have to confront her; to tell her the truth and demand, ask or beg for her help in getting the Iris Stone back. Before it was too late.

And what would that do to them and their brand-new, heartbreakingly vulnerable love?

* * *

Felix Barstow walked through the small hours of the night in the deserted desert town of Tarcoola, towards the train station. He had more than two hours before the *Indian Pacific* was due in, but he was too uptight to be lying in bed in some hotel room, and too angry to be drinking whisky in a bar. Instead he walked moodily down a bereft street, his bag slung over one shoulder, contemplating life with a vicious smile on his face.

He'd never been particularly lucky. Born to middle-class parents, he hadn't had the necessary brains to capitalize on such a promising start by getting into an even moderate university. He wasn't bad looking, but never seemed to have the vital spark which attracted women — let alone wealthy ones from a good family. So he'd fallen into crime almost inevitably, at first without much success, as a two-year stretch in prison for embezzlement showed. But he met people inside who taught him the ways of life, and then put him in touch with other more competent people outside, until eventually he learned enough tricks of the trade to become a freelancer for people in trouble.

People like Greg Nones, who needed some dirty work done — for the right price, naturally.

Now he lived relatively well. He had to be careful of the cops, of course, and even more so of the Inland Revenue. But he could afford good holidays now. And he could buy all the women he wanted. But still, occasionally, he felt as if bad luck continued to plague him, just waiting to make his life miserable. Take this McLeod caper, for instance. It was going bad on him. He could feel it.

When a friend of a friend had introduced him to Greg Nones and pocketed his finder's fee, things had at first seemed so easy. The job wasn't hard — he knew plenty of good forgers, and an arsonist wasn't hard to come by. Setting up the insurance scam had been child's play for someone of Felix's mentality, and when Nones had told him he wanted him to come down under and keep tabs on his business partner, it had seemed the ideal chance to take a bit of a busman's holiday.

But now he wasn't so sure.

He didn't like the way things kept going wrong. The blonde, for a start, wasn't following the game plan he and Nones had worked out for her. Why wasn't she close to nailing McLeod's hide to the wall yet? What had she done with that bloody brochure? She should have told her firm long since, but Greg Nones had heard nothing from the insurance company. And then the Alice Springs gig had gone disastrously wrong.

No, as he walked into the deserted station and slumped onto a bench, Felix Barstow was not a happy man.

He lit a cigarette fretfully and thought about the time difference, then wandered over to a phone. A few moments later, Greg Nones's harsh voice filled his ear.

'It's about bloody time you called. What's going on?'

'Alice Springs was a bust,' Felix said sourly.

'Damn! Things are happening over here too that I don't like. The bank manager was acting oddly yesterday. And I heard on the grapevine that the IRS might be about to pull a spot-check audit on us. I want to move faster than we planned. Look, can you arrange for McLeod to have a little accident? Or even suicide. Suicide might be better.'

Felix grunted. After what had happened in Alice Springs he doubted that any cop worth his salt would buy McLeod's death as either an accident or a suicide. But he was not about to tell Nones that.

'Can do. But it'll cost you another ten grand,' he agreed gruffly.

He listened to the other Englishman squawk and argue, but eventually, as he'd known he must, Nones agreed. Feeling definitely more cheerful now, Felix Barstow hung up. An extra ten grand never hurt. Besides, now it was personal. It felt as if McLeod and his little blonde playmate were laughing at him.

But they wouldn't laugh for long.

* * *

Dane held out his hand as he helped Persis up onto the train. It was still dark, but dawn was threatening its way into the eastern sky as the *Indian Pacific* rolled out of Tarcoola and headed on its longest straight run, towards the west coast and the town of Perth.

'I'm not sure if I want to go to bed for a few hours or not,' Persis said ruefully, as he stood in the doorway of her cabin. 'It's hideously early for breakfast, but I don't feel the least bit tired.'

Dane, knowing he'd never get a better time, closed the door behind him. 'Why don't you have a read of your grandmother's diary? You might find some more clues about . . . Iris,' he urged softly, feeling the pain of his betrayal in every pore of his body and shadow of his soul.

Persis smiled and nodded trustingly. 'If you want, you can stretch out on the bed and take a nap.'

Dane unfolded the main chair into a single bed and slipped off his shoes. Though he lay back, his head was angled down, and his eyes watched her as she unpacked and then settled down on the fold-down stool to read. He watched her turn the pages of the diary restlessly.

'Persis,' he said softly, 'what would you do if you found out that someone you loved had done something . . . wrong?'

Persis tensed and slowly she looked up from the diary, her heart pounding. Was this it? Was he going to tell her what was wrong now?

'What would I do if someone I loved did something wrong?' she heard herself repeating. And felt sick. What had he done? What was so bad that he was scared to tell her? 'Well, I suppose it would depend on what it was,' she said carefully, even as her heart cried out that she didn't care a damn what he'd done — that she'd always love him, no matter what.

Was he not divorced after all? Was he still married? Did he have children? Was he a gambler? Did he have a drink problem? What? She wanted to get up, kiss him and reassure him that it didn't matter what he'd done, she'd always stand by him. At the same time she wanted to get up and shake him and yell at him to tell her. *Just tell her!*

'Oh, nothing criminal. At least, not technically criminal. But if they'd done something morally reprehensible. Something which caused a lot of people a lot of pain. What would you do then?' he pressed. He turned onto his side, propping his hand under his chin and watched her with wary eyes. She really looked up to her grandmother. The way, he supposed, he'd always looked up to his grandfather. There was, he knew, something romantic and appealing about people from a bygone age. People who'd lived when times were so vastly different. But if he was to get the stone back, he would have to shatter her image of Angela, and he knew it would hurt her.

Hence this very careful preparation now. If he could just pave the way a little, and get her to take off her rose-tinted spectacles whenever Angela Canfield-Hope was mentioned, he might just feel better about what was to come.

'I would want to know why this person did whatever it was he did,' she said carefully. 'Did he . . .' She coughed, for her throat had become tight with tension now. 'Did he mean to hurt people, or was it accidental?'

Dane blinked. Now that was a good question. 'I'm not sure,' he said slowly. If you put the best interpretation on Angela's affair with a married man, you could say that she'd been genuinely in love. And love had a way of excusing nearly everything — rightly or wrongly. But he'd personally always seen her as cold-hearted and conniving, simply out to make a buck. Of course, he'd read some of her diary now, and from the little he'd read she'd seemed, at least, human. Perhaps she wasn't the ogre he'd always imagined.

Persis swallowed. She put down the diary and moved towards him, getting down onto her knees to lean against the bed, her face level with his. 'Can't you just tell me what it is?' she said softly. 'I promise, whatever you've done, I'll still love you.'

She watched as a look of utter puzzlement, slowly followed by a dawning realization, crossed his face. 'Me?' he said. Then he laughed. Then, strangely, he looked almost as if he was in pain. 'I wasn't talking about me. But . . .' He trailed off, then slowly, with a look almost of wonderment, reached out to touch her face. 'You really would forgive me, wouldn't you?' he whispered painfully. 'If I *had* done something bad.'

Persis smiled with giddy relief. In fact, she was so overjoyed that he wasn't trying to confess to some hideous sin that it never occurred to her to wonder what he *had* been leading up to.

'Yes, of course I would,' she said simply. 'I love you.'

Dane's jaw clenched. 'I know you do,' he said softly. 'And I love you.'

She nodded, her face shining with happiness.

'No, I mean it,' he said, almost fiercely, as if she'd given some sort of denial. 'I love you. I really do.'

Again she nodded, but looked a little puzzled now.

Dane stared at her helplessly.

What could he do to make her understand? What could he possibly say that in the future, when the whole ugly business about the real 'Iris' came out, would make her still believe in him? Trust that his love was real, and not some trick designed to get behind her defences. What could he do or say that would make her still want him? Because he wasn't sure that he could lose her and still remain intact. To be loved as she loved him, and feel his own love grow in direct proportion, was something new and utterly precious. He had to protect it. He *had* to.

And then he knew. Suddenly, clearly, it came to him.

'Persis Canfield-Hope,' he said softly. 'Will you marry me?'

CHAPTER TEN

The Indian Pacific

Persis took a quick gulp of air and stared at him. 'Wh-what?' she said, rather inelegantly.

Dane smiled, but it was almost a bleak smile. Not the kind of smile, Persis thought with a pang of renewed fear, that a man who'd just proposed marriage should be giving to the woman he loved. 'Are you really so surprised?' he asked, after what seemed to be a silence which had stretched for years.

Slowly, Persis sat back on her heels. He was still lying on his side on the narrow bed, chin propped in one hand, watching her with wary, meadow-green eyes.

'I . . . I'm not sure,' she said. 'I mean, I know it's been quick, our getting together and everything, but . . .' She managed to drag in another breath. 'I know I love you. And you seem to love me.' She felt strangely shy as she talked. She'd never really discussed love with a man before. Certainly not with a man like this one.

'You don't sound too sure,' he said ruefully, but although his lips twisted in a mock-sympathetic smile, his eyes looked full of very real pain.

She frowned. 'I . . . I don't know,' she said at last, to his unspoken question. Did she really believe he loved her? She *wanted* to. And, she laughed deep inside herself, she knew she really *needed* to. But did she? If only she could be sure there wasn't anything holding them back. If only she could even halfway convince herself that there wasn't something standing between them.

He sighed deeply and reached out with his other hand to push back a stray lock of her dark brown hair. 'Poor Persis. This hasn't been much of a holiday for you, has it?' he asked softly. And his gentleness made her want to cry.

'Oh, I don't know,' she said with a brave smile, trying to think of something funny to say but failing miserably. Their eyes met. 'Did you really mean it?' she asked at last, and he nodded.

'Yes. I meant it. Of course, you don't have to decide right away. Marriage is a big step. If you need to fly back home once we reach Perth, I understand. You can always come back again. Or I can fly out to England. We can take our time.'

He was saying all the right conventional things, so why wasn't it making her feel any happier? Or, if the look on his face was anything to go by, why wasn't it comforting him either?

The train continued to sway around them as the miles between them and Perth were slowly but inexorably eaten away. She knew they would be on the train for two days. From her research before starting out, she was well aware that before long they'd be travelling down the longest stretch of straight railway anywhere in the world. From Ooldea to just past Loongana, west of Nurina, was a stretch of over 478 kilometres. Soon trees would become a rarity, although she'd already seen wedge-tailed eagles, more than once, perched on top of telegraph poles.

But somehow, she thought, if the train travelled non-stop for the next hundred days, or even years, she wasn't sure it would be enough time to find out what was wrong between them. She just knew that something was.

‘Are you turning me down?’ Dane asked softly, as the silence stretched to create a gulf between them and she continued to gaze at him, her eyes troubled.

She shook her head fast. ‘No,’ she said, even more quickly. ‘I want to marry you. More than I’ve ever wanted anything else in my life.’ *But.* It hung there between them like the presence of some evil spirit.

Slowly he reached forward and kissed her. Hanging half over the edge of the bed, he put one hand on the vibrating floor of the cabin to steady himself. She moved closer to him, one hand on his shoulder as their lips met and clung. Softly, silently, with lips and tongue and nibbling teeth, they explored each other’s mouths, only slowly and reluctantly pulling apart.

‘I do love you,’ he said softly.

She nodded. ‘All right.’ *But.* There it was again, and abruptly she tossed the but aside and moved closer towards him, coming up onto the bed as he moved back, pushing himself against the wall of the cabin to give her room on the tiny single bed. There they lay, touching along the lengths of their bodies, and slowly he reached out and opened one button on her plain white blouse. She looked down at his meagre progress, then looked back at him.

His dark hair fell in a soft curtain over his forehead, and she idly lifted a finger to brush it back across his scalp. It immediately fell forward again when she removed her hand. She traced the line of his nose with her finger — it was a good nose, strong and straight. Her finger indented over his closed lips then rounded his chin, trailed down his throat and ended at his own shirt button. Wordlessly she undid it.

He smiled, and undid another button of hers.

She smiled back, and undid his second button.

He came to the end of buttons before she did and when it came to her turn, shucked off his shirt. In the confined space it was awkward and he twice bumped his elbows against the wall, but he didn’t so much as wince. She, being on the outside of the bed, had an easier time taking off her blouse.

He slowly reached to slip one finger under the strap of her bra and twanged it gently before sliding his hand around between her shoulder blades and, with a cunning little movement, unhooking it. The lacy cups sagged against her breasts, and with a wriggle of her shoulders, the bra fell down between them. He lifted it in his hands, feeling the warmth of it, loaned from her flesh, and felt his heart leap in response to the small, tender intimacy.

'I really do love you,' he repeated hoarsely. 'I've never loved any woman the way I love you. And I know I never shall.'

Persis kissed the top of his arm nearest to her, before any sign of a 'but' could leap into her mind. He reached forward and planted a kiss where her neck met her shoulder. Then, with his little finger, he brushed the back of his knuckle against her nipple. Instantly, the button of flesh sprang to attention and began to ache.

She moaned a soft-voiced protest.

As if reading her mind, he leant forward and sucked the aching appendage into his mouth. Her eyes feathered closed as radiating waves of tension shot out and installed themselves in every pore of her skin, every muscle, every sinew, leaving her throbbing all over. Even her toes seemed to ache with want of him.

He leaned over her and his hand moved under her skirt, tracing the curve of her knees, then her thighs, then moving to the place where her legs met. She was warm and wet and waiting for his finger, which found her clitoris through the plain white cotton of her briefs and rubbed. Hard. She gasped, moaned, and opened her legs wider. He rolled over her further, his mouth dipping to hers, his tongue caressing her, as his finger rubbed harder and harder. She had to wrench her mouth free in order to gulp in great gasps of air as her body squirmed beneath his knowing hands, until finally she shuddered and lay still.

Then, slowly, her hand moved to the hard ridge which pressed against his trousers, and she began to knead, and not gently. He threw his head back, which hit the cabin wall, but again he didn't make so much as a murmur. Instead both of his hands splayed out against the wall behind him, leaving him open and defenceless against her knowing hand. She rubbed him harder, feeling his trousers grow tighter and tighter, until she undid his belt and slipped her hand between the denim of his jeans and the white silk of his boxer shorts.

He hissed in his breath, stretching like something about to take off, and groaned her name.

She wriggled out of her panties, aware of him pulling down his jeans, and then suddenly she was beneath him, opening herself to him, feeling him fill her with a power which was almost frightening. The train swayed around a bend, and the noise of the engine was a mere dull throb, echoing the sound of her own body's engine. She hooked her legs behind his as they rocked and thrust, climbing higher and higher, tension tightening into ever decreasing circles until she was crying out his name, and she could feel his collapsing body, heavy but satisfying, covering her own.

For a while she lay listening to his gasping breaths as they stilled to a more quiet rhythm in her ear.

Then she slept.

When she woke up he was dressed and sat casually on the floor, leaning back against the door, his arms dangling between his bent knees. His hair was mussed, and he was staring at her. He looked devastatingly handsome. For a second, before he realized she was awake and watching him, she caught the unguarded look on his face.

He looked desperate. And despairing.

Then he noticed her watching him and instantly the shutters came down. He smiled. 'Morning. Ready for something to eat?'

She wasn't, but glanced at her watch, saw that it was nearly ten, and nodded. 'I'll meet you in the dining car,' he said, getting up and leaving her in peace to wash and dress.

She got up slowly, her body aching in that delightful way which always told a woman when she'd been loved well, and splashed water onto her face. She changed into an aqua silk sundress and brushed her teeth and hair.

She couldn't quite meet her reflection in the mirror.

* * *

Felix Barstow was finishing his breakfast when a beautiful brunette walked into the restaurant car. He'd seen her around before, but hadn't paid much attention. He'd had other things on his mind. Besides, she'd been too thin and pale to really attract him. Now, though, she looked ravishingly lovely. Her skin had turned a peach-bronze shade which complimented the colour of her dress and the dark luxuriance of her hair. She seemed to be a little less angular too — less distressed-looking and more healthy. But her eyes flickered over him without interest, then lit up. He turned, watching as a tall man, who could only be an Australian, stood up as she approached, and he shrugged and smiled grimly.

Oh well.

He threw down his napkin and left the car, walking along the swaying corridors with the ease of a man now at peace with a perpetually moving environment. He paused as he passed one of the exterior doors and gave it a quick examination. Electric. Damn. In the old days, there would only have been a handle, and a man had merely to press down on it and hey presto. But since so many attempting suicide had done so by throwing themselves from speeding trains, and since a number of fatal accidents had occurred from people accidentally stumbling into exterior doors and falling, train companies now preferred electronically secure doors which could be operated only from the driver's cabin. Or in case of emergency.

He leaned forward and checked the machinery around the door. It looked simple enough. Although he was by no means an electronics expert, he knew enough to get by. He should be able to rig one of the doors to open from a remote on his key-chain. Just a question of getting online to find out what specifics the makers of the train had installed. It was wonderful what information was available to your local average villain nowadays.

Then all he had to do was pick the exterior door nearest to McLeod's cabin, rig it up to open at his command, and wait. Felix could do that. When he needed it, he had the patience of a fishing heron.

* * *

Persis sighed and turned the page. Sometimes her grand-mother's writing was hard to make out. This sentence here, for instance. Did it read 'Walter took me to Golden Mile' or did it read 'Walter gave me a Golden Smile'?

She checked the top of the page, saw the date — 15 November 1938 — and the place name. Kalgoorlie. So much of her romance with her Walter C seemed centred in Kalgoorlie.

> *I love him so. And, after last night, I know how much he loves me. But I can't accept his gift. He must know I can't. But I can't bear to leave him either. And yet I must. Soon, I must return to England. But I shall leave him my love behind.*

Persis sighed and closed the diary, and the haunting, beautifully written words faded back into the decades already gone by.

She'd leave him her love behind.

Was that what was going to happen with her and Dane, Persis wondered with a fresh wave of despair. Despite his proposal of marriage, and despite the fact that there was no world war to come between them, would she be returning to England soon, leaving nothing but her love behind? Leaving everything behind, in fact?

She glanced up as the door opened and casually tossed the diary onto the table top. She smiled as he looked in.

'Want to come and bird-watch with me? We're about to reach the eastern boundary of the Nullarbor. Nothing but miles of rolling red sand dunes and wedge-tailed eagles.'

'Love to,' she said softly.

As he stepped aside to let her pass, his eye fell to the diary. If only he could photograph those pages, he knew he'd have the answers he sought. But it would take time. And he'd have to be very careful.

'Why don't we get a drink from the bar first,' he murmured. Perhaps a few glasses of wine would make her drowsy. He could then take her back to his cabin and let her sleep, then slip back here and photograph the diary.

As he put a hand on the small of her back, and she turned and looked lovingly up and around at him over her shoulder, he wished she would just spit in his face.

It might make him feel better.

* * *

Felix Barstow stood up and lounged casually against the door as a steward walked by. He nodded and smiled, waited until the coast was clear, and then bent quickly back to his work on the door. A few wires here, a snip there, a check on the microwave frequency used and it would be done.

A few minutes later he tested it. By modifying the now-defunct remote control which had previously unlocked his top-of-the-range Beamer, he should have cracked it.

He pointed the car remote at the exterior door, held his breath and pushed. The door opened. As it did so, however, an alarm began to beep, loud and insistently.

He swore and hastily bent down to fix it. Behind him he heard a cabin door open as someone, somewhere, poked their head out, no doubt to see what all the fuss was about. But Felix didn't care about nosy passengers. He'd once apprenticed himself to a conman, who'd taught him all he needed to know about off-the-cuff patter. If some nosy parker came calling he could easily convince them he was a member of the staff, or even just some on-holiday electrician who'd been asked to help out with a minor fault.

But after a few seconds he managed to locate and neutralize the alarm. And nobody had come asking questions. Now he just had to wait and see if the alarm had sounded in the driver's cabin. If a red warning light had flashed on the engineer's panel saying a door was open while the train was in motion, sooner or later a real member of the train's staff was bound to be along.

He thought, though, that he'd got to it in time. At least the door was now shut and as innocent-looking as a lamb. He retreated to the nearest loo, however, and with the door ajar, waited and watched. Sure enough, a steward did come, looked at the door cautiously, rattled and pulled on it with growing confidence, then went away again, no doubt to report to his superior that all was well. Just a blip in the system. Happened every day, probably.

Felix grinned and went, whistling, back to the bar. It was now only a matter of time before Avery McLeod went hurtling from the train. With a bit of luck, dingoes or lizards or whatever was out there in the Australian bush would even dispose of the body for him. He'd simply vanish from the face of the earth. He might even make it into one of those books which charted mysterious happenings. The mystery of the man who vanished from a train. The Great Australian Mystery. He could almost see the headlines now.

Felix smiled into his scotch and felt positively happy.

* * *

Rayne, hearing an alarm, had trotted to the door of her cabin, but after a few moments, the annoying wail had stopped. Now she shut her door and went back to typing up her report. It was just a quick follow-up after her phone call with Matt, as she knew her boss liked to have a hard copy of the facts, for reference. She sent it via email and switched off the laptop. Next, she checked her watch. Nearly lunchtime.

Time to roust Avery from his cabin and feed him.

* * *

Persis dozed. She was aware, vaguely, of having had a little too much wine with lunch, and as the train hit a slight bend in the tracks and swayed, she guiltily forced open her eyes. She was lying on Dane's bed and he was leaning against the fold-down table, reading a newspaper. He looked up at her and smiled tightly.

'I'm fine,' he whispered bleakly. 'You don't have to entertain me. Take a nap.'

* * *

Dane turned the pages of Angela Canfield-Hope's diary, making sure to get a clear shot of each. He'd ring his grandmother at the next short stop and tell her about it — it would give her hope. He needed to make sure that she hung on long enough for him to place the Iris Stone in her hand.

* * *

Persis woke with a start. She sat up, feeling a little disorientated. Like most people coming into awareness after being asleep, she felt somewhat lost. Then her mind cleared. Of course, she was in her cabin on the train. Except that . . . no, she wasn't. She was in *Dane's* cabin. She glanced at her watch, and wondered where he could be. In one of the bars, probably. On a train, if you didn't want to get claustrophobic in your own tiny cabin, you had to make the most of the recreational public cars.

She got up and grimaced at the furriness of her tongue. Her head, too, began to pound. Yes. Definitely too much wine with lunch. Although, with all the pills she was still taking, her doctors had told her she could only have two glasses of wine per day, in reality she hardly ever drank at all. And the Australian white Dane had chosen had tasted pretty potent. No wonder she hadn't been able to keep her eyes open.

She went to the sink and wondered if it was safe to drink the tap water. Probably. She wasn't, after all, in the depths of a malaria swamp or a Third World country. Then she saw a bottle of mineral water standing on the tiny shelf which passed for a bathroom, and with a smile of thanks at her absent lover, reached for it and poured herself a glass. Did he have aspirin? There were none in the bathroom, so she went to the wardrobe to check his pockets. He was the kind of man who was always prepared — like the boy scouts. She grinned as she felt a foil and plastic strip in the top pocket of his best jacket and pulled her hand out.

Yes. Aspirin.

Who says she didn't know Dane Culver all that well? Triumphantly, she took two aspirin, washed them down, and returned the pills to his pocket. As she did so, she frowned. Why wouldn't they slip back down where she'd found them? Then she realized she was putting them back in the wrong pocket. She pulled her hand out, and as she did so, a much-folded, almost tissue-soft piece of paper came out with it and floated to the floor.

At first, as she bent down to retrieve it, she thought that that was what it was — a tissue. Then she saw with amazement that it wasn't a tissue at all but a yellowed, old, much-handled letter. Over the years, all the handling had given it a nap which resembled the soft skin of a peach.

Why was Dane going around with such an old letter?

She stared at the piece of paper in her hand, suddenly at war with herself. Of course she couldn't unfold it and read it. That was unthinkable. Nobody went around reading other people's private papers.

So why was she still holding it?

Because something was telling her that it was important. But surely that was all the more reason not to read it? She simply couldn't invade his privacy like that. But what if it was important to *her*? What if this piece of paper contained the answer to the puzzle that was Dane? Suppose it contained the answer to the riddle that was their strange, strained courtship. But how could it be?

Without really realizing it, her fingers were unfolding the paper. She stopped. No — it was too awful. She started to move, determined to put the letter back into the pocket, but then two words seemed to leap off the page and stare at her.

Walter C.

Persis blinked. No. It couldn't be. She didn't have any of her grandmother's letters with her. Besides, as far as she knew, her grandmother hadn't written any letters which mentioned her Australian lover. The ones she'd found in the attic after leaving hospital had all been written to her sisters, and made no mention of her escapades in the land down under. Besides . . . As she stared down, mesmerized at the paper, she realized the handwriting wasn't the same as her grandmother's at all. And that Walter C came at the end of the page. It was, in fact, his signature. Not a letter written to him, or about him, but *from* him.

And yet, how could that be?

Slowly, her eyes moved to the top. And she began to read.

My dearest Angela,

I know it's no good writing to you. I'm not sure I'm even going to post this letter. This damned war seems determined to keep us apart. Reading about the bombing in London scares me. Why haven't you written?

I think, my darling, I know why. I just can't bring myself to believe it. And so I'm writing to you. Again.

Ever since our time together in Kalgoorlie, when I took you, my darling, down into the deepest depths of my heart, I've been thinking of you. Think of me too, wherever you are.

All of my love, darling, for always,

Walter C.

Persis stared at the signature for some time before slowly folding the letter and putting it away, careful to return it to the proper pocket. It suddenly seemed vastly important that Dane should never know she'd read it.

Dane.

Why was it in his pocket? Where had he got it? Obviously, Walter C had guessed, even at the time of writing it, that her grandmother had perished in the Blitz. So he'd written it, and kept it, never meaning to send it.

The thought of it made Persis want to cry. To think, all those decades ago, a man on one side of the earth had written of his love, to his love, on the other side of the earth, knowing in his heart she was already gone.

She shook her head and sank down onto the edge of the bed. But still, it made no sense. Why would Dane, of all people, have a letter from Walter C? Slowly she began to grow cold. Then to shiver. A while later she felt a drop of water on her hand, and realized it had fallen from her eyes. She hastily wiped them and shook her head.

Think, damn it, Persis, think. Sitting here weeping was going to do her no good at all.

Dane must know Walter C. Or know of him. So Dane had probably always known about Angela. Now she came to think of it, hadn't he always encouraged her to read about her? And talk about her? All those questions he'd asked about her grandmother, and her grandmother's family and heirs.

So, what were the chances that they'd just *happened* to meet, back in that Sydney café? Had just chanced to be on the same train, and by sheer coincidence struck up a relationship? She shook her head. One who knew Angela Canfield-Hope, and one who knew — in some way or other — her lover of all those years ago, the mysterious Walter C, hadn't, *couldn't have*, just happened to meet.

Walter C. Walter Culver? Was he Dane's relation? But, if that was the case, why hadn't he just said so? She'd told him all about Angela, after all. One thing was for sure — she'd been right about the letter holding the key to their courtship. For some reason, Dane had sought her out.

She had to find out what that reason was. She almost cried out as her heart contracted in pain, cringing from the thought which suddenly telescoped into the most important thing in all the world.

She had to find out if all of this had been a lie.

For if their chance meeting had been a lie, who was to say that the kisses weren't also lies? The love-making? Even the proposal?

She got up and staggered to the door, like someone drunk, and made her way numbly to her cabin. Her room was empty. Gratefully, she closed the door and leaned against it, gasping in air like a fish out of water.

Her eyes went immediately to the table and her grandmother's diary. It wasn't there. Her eyes shot around the room and saw it at once — on the bed. But she knew she'd left it on the table.

'Oh, Dane,' she said softly. 'Oh, Dane!' she wailed.

And throwing herself down onto the bed, she began to weep. Bitterly.

CHAPTER ELEVEN

The Indian Pacific

Avery finished washing and checked his newly shaved face in the mirror. He and Rayne were going to go into the first sitting at dinner, then have an early night at his place. He grinned at the thought of them cooped up in his cabin. At any other time, the thought of spending more than twelve straight hours with one person in such a tiny space would be enough to drive a person insane. But when your playmate was Rayne, and when you had something much more interesting to do than play cards or talk, it was amazing how such a proposition could begin to look downright attractive.

He grinned at himself as he shrugged into his dazzlingly white dress shirt and reached for his black jacket. He glanced at his watch. Nearly 6.30. Rayne should be waiting for him in the dining car by now.

He opened the door and stepped out. At this time of day, the train's corridors were deserted as most people were either changing for dinner in their cabins or drinking aperitifs in the bar. He slipped out and closed the door behind him, vaguely aware as he did so of a man walking up behind him. He turned to face the dining car and set off.

A few yards in front, an exterior door rattled a little as the train went over a point. The man behind Avery began to close the gap between them. Fast.

* * *

Rayne checked her appearance in the mirror and nodded. The little clingy number in mint-green showed off her deepening tan to perfection. She added a green sparkling hair slide to one side of her head, and smeared on some green eyeshadow. A quick squirt of Christian Dior's Dune at both wrists and behind her ears, and she was ready.

As she stepped outside into the deserted corridor, she realized, after a quick glance at her wristwatch, that she was early. She'd go and meet Avery outside his cabin, which was nearer to the dining car anyway.

* * *

In her cabin, Persis reread her grandmother's entries for her time in Kalgoorlie. It was here that her beloved Walter C had given her something that she couldn't possibly accept, along with a golden smile, and where — according to Walter's own letter — he had taken Angela to the deepest part of his heart.

But despite her scrutiny she could make nothing of it. All she knew was that Dane had some kind of a link to what had happened to her grandmother all those years ago, and she was determined to get to the bottom of it all. And that meant deciphering the diary and, more importantly, losing Dane in Kalgoorlie so that she could explore the town and try and find out what was going on, on her own. Because she was beginning to think that Dane was never going to tell her what it was himself. And, what's more, she thought, with her heart aching dully in her chest as she did so, she wasn't sure that she'd believe him if he did.

Or trust him.

* * *

Avery was just passing the exterior door when he heard a slight beep. The kind a man's watch might give as it hit the hour, perhaps, or that of a very muted pager. Then he felt a sudden and ferociously strong hot draught, and as he started to turn his head, surprised by movement in his peripheral vision, he saw the exterior door was beginning to slide open. He just had time to register the slight hissing sound it made, indicative of an electronic rather than a manual door control, when he felt something cannon into him from behind.

His first thought was that it must be a fellow passenger, caught off-balance by the train's motion and accidentally stumbling into him. But the forward motion was too hard, too pronounced and . . . what's more, it wasn't stopping!

He yelled, 'Hey, watch out!' as he felt the weight of the person behind him shoving him sideways, towards the now fully open door. Too late, he realized that this was no accident, and that the door opening mid-journey was no coincidence.

He tried to dig his feet into the ground, but on the flat, shiny surface of the corridor floor, his shoes could get no purchase, and he slipped and slid helplessly. He was heading for the door, and there was nothing he could do to stop it. It was happening so fast. Desperately he shot his hands out sideways, making like a scarecrow, knowing in some scrambling, shocked part of his brain that his only chance of staying inside the train was to catch on to either side of the open doorway and hang on, literally, for dear life.

It was then that the man behind him thumped him viciously in the back, making him cry out as the pain ricocheted around his kidneys. Instinctively he pulled his arms in and crouched over.

Felix Barstow, with a grin of triumph, gathered his strength together for the final push.

* * *

Rayne had just stepped through one of the train's many inter-connecting doors when she heard a noise. At first she thought it was probably kids playing about, as the sound belonged more to the scream-yell-shout category than to any kind of adult conversation. She kept walking, keeping a wary lookout for fast-footed youngsters, not relishing the thought of getting sticky fingers or a half-eaten ice cream smeared all over one of her best dresses.

Then she heard the noise again. And this time there was no mistaking it. A dull 'thump' sound preceded it, and the yell which followed was full of pain. Moreover, it was the sound of an adult man.

Her heart kicked into overdrive and suddenly she was running. She almost crashed through the next door, and as she did so, her heart nearly stopped. For, just in front of her, being propelled through the open door of the train, was Avery.

He was half-crouched in obvious pain, and the man behind him had a white-knuckled grip on the top of both of his arms, preventing him from getting a grip on the door frame.

Her first instinct was to yell and scream and rage at the man to stop, but in the very instant it was born, it died again. She knew that this was the man who'd almost killed them in Alice Springs. This was the man Greg Nones must have hired to kill his partner. And he wasn't going to stop just because she, Rayne Fletcher, yelled her damn fool head off.

She'd never stopped running all during this thought process, but now she deliberately and determinedly picked up speed, her small, fit body hurtling forward as her strong legs pumped like a professional athlete motoring down a race track, prior to taking off for the long jump.

Her eyes wild, her mind raced.

Avery, aware that his head was almost through the door now, dragged his thoughts away from the pain in his back. The desert flashed by outside — a mass of red interspersed with close flashes of vertical brown, which were the telegraph poles that ran alongside the track. He had to stop his forward motion somehow. His hands scrambled out again, but someone was holding his arms pinned to his side, preventing him from grasping the edges.

He was going to die.

The thought seemed to slow everything down. From a muck sweat, where he couldn't quite make himself believe this was happening to him, he seemed to go to ice-cold clarity, all within a nanosecond. His brain, sensing imminent extinction, began to function, to co-operate in finding a solution to his survival, instead of merely sending out panic-stricken, worthless messages.

OK, he was going to die if he went through this open door. The train was probably going at well over seventy miles per hour, and all he had to break his fall were hard unforgiving iron rails and layer upon layer of gravel and hard pebbles and stones. His body would be broken and torn to pieces. He couldn't use his arms to stop him going through, so what did that leave?

His legs.

Before he was even aware of giving the command, his brain synapses fired and he fell to his knees. Which was good in that it stopped dead his headlong flight through the door. But bad in the fact that he was already half out, and only his shins and the tops of his feet hit the corridor floor. The projection of his knees, however, met nothing but thin air.

A hand began to shove down hard between his shoulder blades, propelling him forward mercilessly. His arms, though, had become free, as his sudden downward motion had caught his attacker by surprise. But even as he realized this, he began to roll forward like a wheel, and his view of the flashing-past desert was suddenly transformed into that of the flashing-past railway tracks directly below him.

Diesel and oil darkened the stones in spots as the train sped on its way to the Australian west coast.

His arms shot out, and his fingernails broke painfully as they attempted to scrabble a hold on the unforgiving metal plates at either side of the open door. If only there was a handle, something solid he could grab hold of. But there wasn't.

The hand on his shoulder blades pressed down and forward with renewed, murderous vigour, pushing him ever further out. The toes of his shoes squeaked on the flooring as they scrabbled for purchase.

He wasn't going to be able to stop this.

He didn't dare let go of his tenacious but futile grasp of the door sides to try and reach around behind him and wrestle with his attacker, but he knew he didn't have the strength to hold on much longer. Already the force of gravity, the weakening strength in his arms, and the sheer momentum of his attacker's weight, were making him bend double, so that his nose was almost pressed right down against the outside of the train, beneath the door's opening. Worse, he could feel the toes of his shoes sliding along the corridor. Soon, more of his legs would be outside than in, and then it would all be over.

He cursed, something hard and vicious, but he seemed to have little breath left in his lungs. Desperately, he dragged in a deep breath, tasting hot air and diesel and the even ranker, vile taste of defeat.

Regret flashed through him. He'd never know who wanted him dead or why. Worse, much worse, he'd never see Rayne again. He'd never get to marry her and have those kids he'd wanted. Never get to grow old with her, and tease her about dyeing her hair or exercising. He'd never get to taste his silver or golden wedding anniversary cake with her.

Never make love to her again. It was all gone, and an ineffable sadness washed over him, replacing fear, replacing even the anger.

Oh, Rayne.

He felt his fingers, which had begun bleeding from the broken nails, slide down the metal framing the doors, his own blood turning traitor and making him lose his last tenuous grip on the metal.

This was it.

Then he heard a scream — a high-pitched, furious, avenging yell that turned his blood cold. Was that him?

No. It wasn't.

Rayne, who was now all but on top of the two desperately struggling figures, had decided it was time for a bit of psychological warfare, and let rip with a yell which could strip wallpaper. She'd been taking self-defence lessons for years; not that it was a prerequisite of her job exactly, but she knew that her boss preferred to promote insurance investigators who could take care of themselves. She'd also listened to her instructor's after-class lessons.

Gavin Westcott was rumoured to be ex-SAS, but he'd never confirmed or denied this to any of his class. Nevertheless, he had most definitely been in the army, and more than once had dropped pearls of wisdom into the ears of his students, as they'd joined him at the local bar for a drink. And one of his tips had been how a loud sound, at the right moment, could paralyze an enemy long enough to give you a tiny but distinct advantage.

And it worked now.

Felix Barstow jumped as a foghorn seemed to sound in his ear. Instinctively, he lessened the pressure on Avery's shoulders, jumping back a little and looking around.

It was his first mistake.

A flying foot caught him squarely under his chin, lifting him up and back, his hold on Avery going completely.

Avery, feeling the sudden lack of pressure on his back, found himself rearing back uncontrollably, as all his strength had been concentrated on resisting the forward pressure. Consequently, he now found himself catapulted up, which made him hopelessly overbalance, losing his grip on the sides of the door completely.

He gave a yell as he felt himself falling.

Rayne, alerted, took her eyes off Felix long enough to see her lover sliding over the edge.

Quickly she reached for his legs and pulled hard.

She cursed then saw that Avery had one hand at least on the side of the door again, and had no other choice but to let go, spinning up and around to face Felix Barstow — who was already lunging towards her, snarling.

His second mistake.

Thanks to her training, Rayne knew exactly what a smaller, weaker combatant needed to do when faced with a charging, superior force. Namely, use that superior force against her attacker.

Felix just had time to see the tight, grim, unafraid face of the blonde insurance investigator go perfectly blank before it dipped and went out of sight. What the . . . ? He was still moving forward, and suddenly she was under him. Her turned shoulder connected with his stomach, expelling the air from his lungs in a painful *whoosh*.

Then he was airborne. He wasn't aware how, only that he was turning, his world becoming upside down; and now the hot air of the flying train was tugging at his clothes, causing his shirt to billow and making snapping noises all around him.

His last sight was that of Avery McLeod, disappearing back inside the train.

* * *

Avery lay on his side, his chest heaving. Knelt beside him, one hand protectively on his arm, Rayne was sobbing over him.

'It's all right,' she murmured mindlessly, over and over. 'Just breathe. It's all right.'

Eventually, Avery slowly rolled over onto his back. One hand still hung outside the train, moving up and down with the force of the wind. He opened his eyes and saw her face above him, blue eyes filled and overspilling with tears.

Rayne. Of course. Who else?

'You're so damned beautiful,' he said hoarsely. His mouth was so dry, the words came out like the croaking of a frog. But Rayne had never heard any sound so wonderful. She laughed, sniffed, then wiped her eyes with the back of her hand.

'Course I am,' she said cheekily.

Slowly, with his breathing returning to normal, he swallowed hard once or twice. Then, feeling stiff and sore all over, he managed to scramble onto his backside and sit with his back braced against the wall, his legs still shaking with shock.

Opposite him, Rayne did the same, equally shaking all over. The open doorway between them continued to mesmerize them with the flash of red desert, vertical striations of wooden pole and the grey ribbon of gravel which hugged the railway line. Avery kept looking from it, to her, and back again. Finally, he felt able to talk.

'You saved my life,' he said huskily.

Rayne nodded. 'Yes,' she said simply. 'I was coming to pick you up for dinner and saw you. You were already halfway out, so I ran, yelled, then kicked him under his chin.'

Avery nodded, remembering the sound of the scream — a banshee call coming in the nick of time. That explained how he suddenly got free.

'Then you grabbed my legs and pulled me back,' he said, remembering the tight, life-saving grip around his calves.

She nodded. 'But then I had to let you go. He was coming for me again. Too fast, as it happens. I simply ducked and gave him the old standard roll up and over. And out,' she added, swallowing hard, as it suddenly hit her.

She'd just killed a man.

She glanced at the open door then quickly away again. What had she done? For a second, her whole world seemed to grow dark.

'Rayne!' Her voice, being called sharply, made her jump. Blearily, she managed to focus her eyes on Avery's face. His eyes were dark and knowing. And held hers like a vice. Anchoring her. 'He would have killed me,' Avery said simply. Intensely. And the nightmare receded a little for her.

Yes, Rayne thought, he would have.

And with that, her life seemed to teeter back onto a proper axis again. For, as bad as it felt to be responsible for ending a life, she knew she would have felt infinitely worse if the life which had been lost had been Avery's. And not only because she loved him. But because he was innocent. *He* hadn't been trying to murder anybody else.

'Thank you,' Avery continued softly. 'For saving me. For everything.' Now there would be that life he'd thought he'd lost, after all. Those kids. That anniversary cake.

In that moment, Rayne saw something in his eyes which restored her. She knew that she was going to be able to live with herself, and the events and consequences of the last few minutes, after all.

'I didn't know you knew those kind of moves,' Avery said at last, sensing her need to talk. To be normal. To *feel* normal.

'Oh, it's a part of my job,' she said vaguely, waving a limp hand dismissively in the air. She was suddenly exhausted. While part of her knew that this sudden longing for sleep was due to shock, it was hard to resist, nonetheless.

'What? As a secretary?' he asked, half amused, half alert.

'No. As an insurance investigator for Reut, Cole and Phipps.'

Avery frowned. 'Why does that sound familiar?'

Rayne laughed wearily. 'It should do. They're your insurance company.'

He nodded, one minor mystery solved, and leaned his head wearily back against the wall. Hell, he felt tired. Then he frowned again. 'Wait a minute. Didn't you tell me you worked as a secretary?'

Rayne opened her eyes and looked at him. 'I fibbed.'

'Why?'

'Because I was investigating you,' she heard herself saying hopelessly. 'You were my mark. And it's not standard business practice to tell the people you're investigating that you're investigating them. It tends to make them nervous. Not to mention downright evasive. Definitely not good business tactics at all,' she finished, shaking her head mock-sorrowfully.

But she was too tired, and too stressed, and too shell-shocked to bring off humour, and instead her voice came out flat and disinterested. For a few moments, Avery stared at her blankly. Moments which had her heartbeat picking up fearfully.

The crunch was coming. And never had she felt less equipped to deal with it.

'You were investigating me?' he finally repeated carefully.

Rayne nodded. 'I don't suppose the name Littledore Manor means anything to you, does it?' She watched him closely, more out of habit now than anything, but his face remained utterly blank and uncomprehending. 'Didn't think so,' she said. Then, in an exhausted voice, went on to tell him about Cloud Nine's supposed purchase of the run-down manor, the fire, and the claim for insurance, all in his name.

'But I never put in a claim,' he said, sounding bewildered now.

'*We* know. Your signature was forged.'

Something in her voice — guilt, perhaps, or fear — made him sit up and take better notice. The lassitude that came after surviving imminent death began to fade. Suddenly he was aware that he'd wandered into a minefield of quite a different sort. But one no less explosive. His signature. Faked. Something, somewhere, was buzzing in the back of his mind, warning him that there was something he needed to be concentrating on here.

And, looking at her tense, tired, worried face, he suddenly realized what it was. His eyes opened wide.

'That day you asked me to write down my address and telephone number. You teased me into signing my name . . .' His voice trailed off as he mentally made the connection. 'Even then, you were . . . *investigating* me. You thought I was pulling a scam.'

His voice was hurt. No two ways about it.

Rayne felt her heart slip and slide to the vicinity of her boots. But what else could she expect? 'Yes,' she agreed listlessly.

For a while, Avery stared at her, his mind whirling like a dervish. 'What else?'

'I got your fingerprints from a glass in a restaurant once. But they came in handy,' she added quickly, desperate to come up with some mitigating circumstances in her defence.

'They proved that the brochure I found in your cabin hadn't been handled by you.'

Too late she realized her mistake.

'You searched my cabin?'

She nodded. 'I found a brochure, or rather an incomplete mock-up of one, on Littledore Manor. I sent it back home, but it came up clean. That was one of the factors which convinced me and my boss that you were clean. That Greg Nones was behind it all.'

Her voice was all but hopeless now. With every word she spoke she seemed to be hammering another nail in her own coffin.

'So, when we met . . .' he began, then swallowed hard and tried again. 'When we met, it was all prearranged. You *meant* to hook up with me.' She hadn't been attracted to him at all. Hadn't wanted him. Hadn't, probably, even liked him much. She had just been doing her job.

'Right,' she agreed flatly.

'And all the time we were together, you were watching me, thinking . . .'

'Thinking up ways to prevent your "claim" being met by us, yes,' Rayne said, close to tears again, but determined not to shed them. He deserved more from her than that. 'There was even a promotion in it for me if I could bring it off,' she added, wondering why she was feeling so compelled to be honest and paint herself in the worst possible light. Was it really just bull-headedness? The old, might-as-well-be-hung-for-a-sheep-as-a-lamb mentality? Or was she just too tired to lie anymore? Or, much more likely, did she just feel that she owed this decent, wonderful man the truth at last?

Grimly, she explained about her being in a two-horse race for a promotion which, if won, was bound to lead to her being offered a partnership at Reut, Cole and Phipps.

As she talked, Avery felt his heart begin to ache. She was describing a whole world he knew nothing about; a job which she was obviously so very good at. What else waited for her back home in England that he knew nothing about? A boyfriend? A husband, even?

'So when we were nearly killed in Alice Springs,' he heard her say, and realized she was still talking, 'my boss and I got together and figured on Greg Nones. Which reminds me — I've got to call England. And then the police at the next stop. Where is that? Haig? They'll want to know where to find his body,' she said, nodding grimly at the still-open door. 'And send someone out to recover it.'

She glanced at her watch, desperate to distract herself from the fact that she'd probably just lost the only man she'd ever loved. 'I figure he went out at about a quarter past six. Given the train's speed at roughly seventy miles per hour . . .'

Avery did the mental arithmetic and helped her out, giving his calculations. She nodded a thanks and got wearily to her feet. He too scrambled up on legs which felt like jelly. 'I'll have to inform someone on the train too,' she added. 'There has to be someone in charge of security on board.'

She was sounding all crispness and authority now, and again Avery felt her slipping further and further away from him. Gone was his saucy, cheerful, wonderfully pretty Rayne. Soon, they'd be in Kalgoorlie and the case would be over for her. She'd fly home to England.

And he . . . he'd have lost her. No, that was not quite right, he thought, wanting to just slump back down onto the floor and cry.

He'd never really had her.

CHAPTER TWELVE

Kalgoorlie

The train pulled in at Kalgoorlie-Boulder on its twice weekly crossing of the continent right on time, and Persis was nearly the very first to get off. As she did so, she noticed three policemen looking quickly along the length of the train, their faces tight and alert, before boarding.

She wondered, briefly, who they'd come to see, or maybe even arrest. Then she shrugged. It was none of her business. She had problems of her own. She'd managed to keep Dane in his own cabin last night by pleading tiredness and a headache, and he'd been at once contrite and solicitous. It had taken her a few moments to realize that he was still concerned with her convalescence, whereas she herself, for the first time since falling ill, had all but forgotten about her spell in hospital, and all the wearying months of illness which had followed and been so much a part of her life. In fact, when she'd seen him out of her cabin the night before, she realized that she'd felt, physically at least, totally recovered.

This morning, and for the rest of the day on the train, however, she'd managed to keep up the pretence of there being nothing wrong, although periodically she'd felt the urge to shout at him, to accuse him of reading her grandmother's diary and demanding to know why he was so curious. At other, calmer times, she wondered if he was truly related to Walter C. And if, as she supposed, his ancestor and her own had created a child together, did that make them distantly related?

She'd barely picked at her lunch, having no appetite, and had in fact taken a nap that afternoon, not out of any sense of fatigue but merely so that now she would be refreshed and ready. Ready to do what she knew she must.

She figured it would take Dane a few minutes to get to her cabin, knock, and discover that she was gone. So she'd have to be quick. The moment the train pulled into the station, she was out, her bags beside her. She wasted what felt like precious minutes finding the luggage lockers and stowing them away, and as she hurried outside into the evening heat and dusty air, she glanced nervously over her shoulder.

The station was crowded, of course, but she could see no sign of Dane. With a twinge of unease, she wondered what she was going to tell him when he caught up with her later, but she could always use the excuse that she'd lost him in the crowd.

As she stepped onto the street and hailed a taxi, she wondered, with even more unease, if any excuse would, in the end, even be necessary. Something was telling her that all the answers were waiting for her here, in Kalgoorlie, and that they might not be the ones she wanted.

She was still clinging stubbornly to the hope that she and Dane had a future together, but what if they didn't?

Quickly, she thrust the thought aside. Whatever it was that Dane was hiding, it couldn't be that bad, surely? Nothing was unconquerable when people loved each other. Firmly telling herself that, she asked the taxi driver to take her to the public library, hoping that it would still be open this late.

She didn't see the tall figure of a man walk quickly from the shade of the station where he'd been watching her, and get into the next cab in line.

Dane Culver slammed the door behind him.

'G'day, mate. Where to?' the taxi driver asked cheerfully.

'Follow the cab in front,' Dane said tersely, and was instantly transported back to Sydney, when all of this had first started. He'd felt disgruntled and foolish then, following Persis Canfield-Hope about like some second-rate private eye. He still felt so now. Only now he felt something else as well.

Fear.

Why had she given him the slip? He'd arrived at her cabin just in time to see her disappear into the connecting corridor ahead, and had instinctively scented danger. And when he'd hurried after her and seen that she was carrying her bags, he knew it was justified. Why had she left her cabin before the train had even stopped, and be carrying her own luggage, unless she meant to be one of the first to get off? And on the station, when he'd watched from behind a newspaper stand as she'd stowed her luggage in a locker, he knew she was definitely in a hurry to be free. And probably had no intention of heading to the hotel he'd pre-booked for them, either.

Also, the way she'd kept looking around, checking for someone — someone who could only be him — made him convinced that something was up. Something, somehow, had changed.

But what?

As the taxi drew away, the driver giving his passenger an interested, slightly wary look, Dane drummed his fingers tensely on his knees. What if she'd always planned on dodging him here? What if she'd known all along where the Iris Stone was. Who he was. What if she had been a superb actress all this time, laughing at him behind that lovely face of hers.

He took a breath and mentally shook his head. No. He couldn't think like that. Couldn't bear to.

Ahead, the taxi pulled up at what looked like a public building.

'Here yer are, mate. Funny place to head for, straight off the train, if yer don't mind my saying,' the taxi driver drawled in the broadest Australian accent Dane had ever heard.

'Where is it?' he asked flatly.

'The library, mate.'

* * *

It didn't take Persis long with the microfiche to learn all about Kalgoorlie's history. The gold capital of Australia, the goldrush had been set off by Paddy Hannan's discovery of the wonderful gold metal in 1893. Now, over a hundred years since the discovery, the town was still the site of the world's biggest single open-cut mining operation to recover gold on the Golden Mile.

Golden Mile.

Persis stopped reading the newspaper article, and lifted her head to stare blankly at the wall opposite her. One of the many hard-to-read lines of her grandmother's diary flashed into her mind. Golden smile had to be golden mile. He'd taken her there. Had Walter C, like Dane Culver, been a mine owner here, all those years ago?

Was that the connection between them?

Hastily, Persis sought out the librarian, who was only too happy to help the pretty visitor from overseas. She was so engrossed in her search for any clues that she didn't notice the tall figure slip through the big public doors and silently glide behind a stack of books.

She knew the library closed at nine, and wondered despairingly if she'd have to come back in the morning. Which would mean, somehow, yet again managing to elude Dane. But she was lucky.

Kalgoorlie was proud of its history, and it was well documented. Although she could find no birth, death or even marriage notices for an Iris Canfield-Hope, or even anyone called Iris with a last name beginning with the letter C, she *did* come across a Walter C.

Walter Cartwright, to be precise. And he was indeed a mine owner and operator back between the wars. In fact, not only had Cartwright mined gold, she learned, but he'd also sunk a deep shaft in search of other goodies.

The local newspaper of the time gave no mention about whether or not he found any, albeit this was an early article; if she came back tomorrow and could go through the rest of them there might be more to discover. It did, however, give the name of the mine. Which happened to be, coincidentally, the deepest mine in Kalgoorlie.

The Sweetheart Mine.

The moment she read it, her heart leapt. And as it did so, her mind flashed back to that old, much-thumbed letter she'd found in Dane's cabin. Hadn't he written something about taking her into the deepest part of his heart?

The Sweetheart Mine — the deepest heart in Kalgoorlie.

She went back to the librarian. 'Excuse me, can you tell me if the Sweetheart Mine still exists?'

The librarian looked up, smiling. 'Oh yes, but it closed a while ago. Hasn't been worked for over fifty years.'

Persis smiled. 'It was owned by Walter Cartwright, wasn't it?' she asked winningly. Although the librarian was too young to have been born until well after the war, she was hoping that, in a small town like this, the locals would have learned their history well. Who knew, there might even be someone still living who remembered Walter Cartwright and would be willing to talk to her.

Behind the books, in the quiet and deserted room, Dane could hear every word they were saying. How did she come to suddenly know all about his grandfather? Unless she'd known all along. And why the interest in the Sweetheart Mine?

He felt, suddenly, almost ill.

Back at his desk, the librarian was only too willing to talk. 'Oh yes. Mind you, technically it belongs to Culver Mining now,' he said, pleased to display his knowledge to such a pretty young thing.

Persis felt herself sway and hastily reached out to grab the desk. So much for congratulating herself on being fully over her illness. But she knew, even as she thought it, that this sudden faintness had nothing to do with the lingering effects of her time in hospital. No. This was much more personal.

'Culver Mining,' she managed to repeat with, she hoped, an only vaguely curious voice. 'Oh, did they buy Mr Cartwright out?'

'Oh no — he was family. Old man Cartwright had only one child, a daughter, and she married a Culver. The son, or grandson, runs the whole outfit now. They've still got stakes in town — but not the old Sweetheart Mine,' the librarian said, smiling. 'I doubt anyone's been out that way for years.'

Persis managed a smile.

Dane Culver was Walter C's grandson. And he'd just happened to meet her in Sydney and latch on to her? Somehow, Persis didn't think so. But why? That's what she still couldn't make out. Why? What did he hope to gain? Or was he just curious about her? Had he, too, learned all about his grandfather's great love affair and wanted to . . . what?

Here her logic and reasoning just couldn't help her out, no matter how much she wanted them to. No, there had to be a specific reason for Dane pursuing her. There was still, she knew, a big unanswered question in all of this. She only hoped, oh, how she hoped, that he hadn't been lying about loving her.

'You don't happen to know anyone in town called Iris, do you?' Persis asked, and behind the bookcase, Dane blinked. For a second, he felt stunned. If she was still thinking about Iris in terms of a human being, then . . . He felt a grin spread over his face. If that was so, she still couldn't know about the stolen opal. Things had suddenly gone from looking utterly bleak to something far more resembling a dark cloud with at least the possibility of a silver lining.

'Iris? No, afraid not,' the librarian said, surprised by the sudden change of topic. Persis nodded, disappointed but not surprised. It had probably been too much to hope for. She returned to the microfiche but learned little more.

When she glanced at her watch and saw that it was gone eight, she rose stiffly. She supposed she should collect her luggage and check in at the hotel. But as she left the library and stepped into the warm mellow evening, she felt reluctant to give up now. She'd learned so much in such a short space of time. When she noticed a taxi turn the corner, she found herself making up her mind and hailed it on impulse.

'Hello. Can you take me to the old Sweetheart Mine,' she asked, getting in, unaware that Dane, who'd just opened the door to the library behind her, heard her request.

'You mean the Hannans North Tourist Mine, don't yer, lady? It's thirty-six metres level underground. But it'll be closed now, I reckon.'

'No. I meant the old Cartwright mine.'

The taxi driver looked puzzled and reached for the radio. As she leaned back in the back seat, Dane raced down the steps, his head swivelling in search of another taxi. But there wasn't one in sight.

On the radio, the taxi driver got in touch with headquarters, where someone, apparently, had heard of the mine. When he hung up, he looked at her in the mirror. 'That's a couple of miles outta town. Nothing out there but dust and spiders, I reckon. And it'll be dark soon. Sure you wanna go out there now, lady?' he asked anxiously.

It sounded stupid, Persis knew. Already she could practically read his mind. A pommie Sheila with no more sense than to go out to deserted mines at night. The sensible thing was to go to her hotel and check it out tomorrow. But she could sense that she was close now. She couldn't give up so tamely.

'I'm sure. But if you have a torch I can borrow, and if you can come back for me, say, after an hour, I'd be really grateful,' she said, and smiled winningly. 'I'll pay extra.'

The taxi driver, perhaps mollified by the thought of the large tip, or perhaps because his male protectiveness had been appeased by the thought of her asking him to return for her, nodded. 'Fair enough,' he said, and put the dusty cab in gear.

And Dane could only watch helplessly as the taxi pulled out of sight.

* * *

The sky was beginning to take on the amber glow that precedes sunset when the cab pulled up on the rutted dirt track. In front of her was the most dilapidated-looking garden shed she'd ever seen. The wooden boards were bleached almost white and hung at drunken angles. There was no other sign, for endless, countless miles, that man had ever been in this particular spot.

'Here yer go,' the driver said, handing over a torch from the front of the cab. 'I'll be back in an hour, sharp. Don't go wandering off into the bush, right?' he said firmly, looking around with renewed nervousness.

Persis gave the miles of unending desert the briefest of glances and smiled grimly. 'Don't worry. I won't.' Encountering snakes and spiders and who knew what else, when she was only wearing flat-heeled sandals and a white sundress which left her legs entirely bare, wasn't high on her agenda of things to do.

The taxi driver looked around the desolate, abandoned spot once more, then back at the gorgeous-looking Sheila in his rear-view mirror, and shook his head. Women. Who could figure them?

Persis got out and then watched the cab drive away. And once the noise of the cheerful engine had faded, found herself feeling suddenly afraid. And alone.

She shivered.

Angry at herself for being so perverse, she walked to the shed and found, of course, that it wasn't a shed at all, but the entrance to a mine. Above the lintel, burned into the wood, she was just able to make out some letters. S–E–HE–T M–NE.

She wondered if Walter had named it after Angela. But of course, he couldn't have. They hadn't met when he'd sunk this shaft. She walked to the dilapidated entrance and saw the padlock at once. Fool! Why hadn't she thought of that? She reached for it, and felt the rust of ages scrape her skin. As she did so, the piece of wood it was attached to came clean away with just a little groan and a splintering of wood. She couldn't help but laugh. So much for security. Mind you, the padlock was still firmly closed! Then she shrugged. What was there to guard, after all?

Nervously she tugged at the rest of the wood, which was so old and dry it all but splintered apart in her hands. Inside, a short, dark, very deeply dipping tunnel was revealed, which seemingly led to the bowels of the earth.

She wasn't really going to go in there, was she?

She checked the torch, and found that it gave a strong white beam. Behind her, the blazing orange sun shone bright and reassuringly warm.

Well, she'd come all this way on a hunch, so why not add one more folly to the list? Besides, there was no sign warning that the mine was condemned or unstable or anything like that. Carefully, she moved forward, crouching to stop herself from hitting her head, but after a while, as the tunnel dipped ever deeper into the earth, she was able to stand fully upright. The light from outside filtered in a fair way, and reassured her even further.

She needn't go far. She needn't, in fact, lose sight of the daylight at all. She was not *that* stupid. Feeling a bit like a heroine from one of those children's books, where feisty teenagers were always up for a grand adventure, she swung the torch beam around, which bounced off old support beams and reddish-coloured, compacted sand. Or was it rock?

Further down, the light was less obvious, but her torch was reassuringly bright. The ground beneath her was hard and unlittered by rocks or boulders. It seemed, in fact, almost incongruously neat. By now she was so far inside that she didn't hear the sound of a second engine as yet another taxi pulled up outside the mine.

After Dane paid off the driver, who looked at him as curiously as Persis's driver had looked at her, he walked straight towards the mine.

As the taxi pulled away, he looked down at the piles of wood on the floor, mute testimony to her larcenous activities, and his lips firmed into a grim line. He peered into the dark hole and wondered just what the hell she thought she was doing. He knew, vaguely, the specifics of the mine, but he himself had never been down it, because it had never been productive. It had just been one more useless or played-out mine which had been part and parcel of the company he'd inherited.

But at least he knew about mines, and their pitfalls and dangers. *He'd* never go down an old and previously abandoned mine without the right equipment, and without telling someone where he was and what time he was expected back. Lives depended on safety issues just such as these.

As he stood there, peering inside, sure that he could make out, just faintly, the light of a torch way ahead of him, he felt a wave of fierce anger wash over him.

What if there was a cave-in? What if she got lost? Was she insane? Without a second thought, Dane plunged in after her.

Ahead of him, Persis began to shiver. It wasn't something she'd ever thought she would do in Australia! But as she moved on, reassured by the fact that, so far, the mine was just this one tunnel, so she couldn't possibly get lost, she realized that the air was not only cold but damp too. She reached out and touched a wall. Although her hand didn't come away clammy or wet, the rock felt cool. Somewhere, she was sure, the mine must run into an underground river or sinkhole or something with water in it.

She moved on, telling herself that if she came to a fork in the tunnel, even if it presented a simple choice of a right or left option, she would turn back. She wasn't going to risk getting lost down here.

But the tunnel merely carried on sinking and boring into the earth. She swung the torch around, checking out the condition of the beams nervously. They looked unrotted and solid enough to her. As her torch beam swept over an overhead section of wooden shoring, she saw writing.

Intrigued, she stood on tiptoe, centring the light of the torch, and reached up to carefully brush away the dirt.

Sam Devereaux. 1938.

She smiled. Even here, in the depths of the earth, in the midst of the great Australian outback, mankind had to leave a mark. She wondered, with a twinge of sentimentality, who Sam Devereaux had been. And even though he was possibly long dead, as her fingertips traced the carved letters of his name, she felt a kinship with him. Had he known, all those years ago when he'd carved his name in the wood, that years in the future, a woman would read his name and smile?

She sighed and moved on, only to stop a minute or so later, sensing something different. Quickly, she swung the beam around, and then realized what it was.

She was standing in a small clearing. Instead of the walls closing in all around her, there was at least six feet of space either side of her. Had they excavated just here for any reason? Her knowledge of geology, and the science of mining, was all but zero. She supposed Dane could have told her all about this unexpected antechamber, if he'd been here.

Dane.

No, she mustn't think about him just yet. She wished, though, that he *was* here. Firmly, she pushed the wish away, and looked around, intrigued. And then she saw it, in the wood — a carved shape. A heart.

Her mind instantly threw up a passage from her grandmother's diary. Something about how her Walter C had carved her initials deep in his heart.

She moved closer, then stopped dead. Had she heard something just then? No. Of course not. What was there to hear down in the quiet earth, far from town and human habitation?

If she thought she'd heard the sound of footsteps other than her own, then she was going mad. Unless she believed in ghosts. Unless she thought that Sam Devereaux still haunted this tunnel in more than name only.

She shook her head, although her heart was hammering and her throat had gone dry. It had sounded like someone walking behind her. A long way behind her perhaps, but footsteps nevertheless.

But it couldn't be.

She moved towards the massive wooden beam which held back one wall of the antechamber. The shape of the heart was still clear, and as she wiped it with her hand, wincing at a splinter which lodged in her thumb, she saw the initials 'A C-H'. And she knew. Sometime, lost in the decades now, Walter had taken a few moments to carve her grandmother's initials in the wood.

She smiled, feeling choked, her earlier, almost supernatural fears now all but forgotten. Here was solid proof of the love of her grandmother's life. Here, right where she now stood, Angela might have watched her beloved Walter C as he carved these letters.

Did he carry a bushman's knife? Had he worn one of those ubiquitous outback hats, sweat-stained and dusty? Had he kissed her? Oh yes, he must surely have kissed her. A hundred yards behind her, Dane paused to listen.

Why couldn't he hear her? From the moment he'd stepped into the tunnel he'd been aware of her up ahead. The movement of her feet on the floor. The ghostly illumination of her torch, providing him with much-needed light. Mostly, he'd been forced to feel his way along the tunnel, using his fingertips as guides. Not that he feared the dark. Or confined, dangerous spaces. But now he felt his heart lurch in very real fear. Had she fallen? Fainted? Taken a fork in the tunnel? If she had, how would he ever find her? He began to move faster, as sure-footed as a cat, sick with fear for her.

In the antechamber, Persis was frowning at the wooden beam. What were those lines surrounding the heart-shaped carving with her grandmother's initials? It looked like a crude square, cut all the way around it. As if someone had tried to cut a square from the wood, containing the lover's message, and remove it. But that made no sense.

She moved closer, running her fingernails in the groove. Yes, it was some sort of a cutting. The years had widened it. And the wood was a little rotten all around the square, where it had been cut.

Rotten.

With a start she realized the air in here was quite moist now. She must be closer to the source of the water. She looked around nervously, but there was no sign of water cascading from the walls. Nevertheless, she wondered when it had last rained here. Or in the nearest mountains. Into her mind flashed scenes from various disaster movies. Weren't the hero and heroine always swept away by events they knew nothing of, happening sometimes hundreds of miles away?

She shook her head. First it was ghosts, now it was some fearsome, non-existent flash flood.

She picked restlessly at the square edges of the cut. Why had Walter done it? If he had. The edges looked rather crude to her, as if someone not used to working with a knife or in wood had hacked at it. Suddenly, a square of wood popped out of the beam and fell onto her foot. She made a small squeak of surprise and stepped back. It was this that covered the appearance of Dane, right behind her, and prevented her from realizing he was there.

In the small opening, from the light of the torch, he was able to see her clearly. He moved forward, about to call her name. And then he saw what she was staring at — the recess carved into one of the support beams.

He moved closer, but stealthily now.

Persis, still unaware of his presence, stared into the dark hole. Perhaps there was a spider in there — one of Australian's many infamous, poisonous kinds. But that was silly. No spider would live in there. Why would it? It was cold, damp, and there was nothing for it to eat. Nevertheless she felt her skin crawl as she slowly lifted her hand. For some reason, either Walter or Angela had made this little cavity in the wood, with the carved heart bearing her initials. And she wanted to know why.

Her skin erupted in gooseflesh as she moved her hand to the opening, drawing her fingers in together in order to be able to narrow her hand enough to get it inside.

Behind her, Dane felt himself go cold. Because, suddenly, he knew what she was going to find in there. And knew too that she must have known of its existence all along. How else had she managed to come here, right to where it lay hidden? In all likelihood, she'd probably come to Australia only in order to retrieve it.

Suddenly, it all made sense.

She hadn't known about the opal until she'd stumbled across her grandmother's diaries. Then she must have put the pieces together, and determined to have the stone for herself.

Despite her seeming ignorance about mining and the Culver name, nothing else made sense or fit so perfectly together. She was obviously a much better actress than Dane had thought.

He felt something, deep inside himself, begin to break.

Persis cautiously splayed her fingertips, wincing as she touched damp wood. Then she gasped as her sensitive fingertips brushed something soft and yielding. With a little gasp she quickly lifted her hand off it. Then she told herself crossly not to be so faint-hearted. And again, cautiously, she lowered her fingers. Whatever it was felt soft and yet . . . something hard was underneath it. She grasped it firmly, making a fist, having to squeeze her hand painfully to get it back out of the hole.

When she did so and looked down at her prize, she frowned in puzzlement. A little drawstring bag, made out of what felt like suede or maybe chamois leather, rested in her hand. It felt heavy. She touched it, moving it around cautiously. It felt as if something round and heavy was inside — like a pebble.

The drawstring was rotten and came apart in her hands, and she had only to turn the little bag upside down to set the object inside free. It tumbled into her palm and lay gleaming against the paleness of her skin. Pale itself. Milky white in fact. Oval, and surrounded by dullish, filigreed metal, it was a piece of jewellery. A necklace.

But it was the stone itself which made her gasp. Big, white, oval.

An opal.

She looked at it, utterly stunned. It was the size of a hen's egg, almost. And that was not all. Inside it, stretching from the longest sides of the ovoid shape in an almost perfectly symmetrical arch, was a rainbow. Literally, a rainbow of colour. Red, gold, green, blue, purple. The artificial light of the torch set the colours gleaming.

'It's a rainbow stone,' she said breathlessly, her voice a hushed, reverent whisper.

'The Iris Stone, in fact,' Dane said grimly.

Persis screamed and whirled to face him.

'And it belongs to us,' he said, his voice as hard as the look in his eyes. And he held out his hand for it imperiously.

CHAPTER THIRTEEN

Kalgoorlie and Perth

Avery walked out of the police station and onto the baking street. A disbelieving glance at his watch confirmed that he'd been at the station all night, answering questions. The fact that he hadn't been arrested probably meant that he wasn't being charged with murder or manslaughter. Or at least, not yet. The inspector who'd questioned him, however, had told him somewhat ironically not to leave town.

His stomach rumbled in hungry protest and he glanced around for a café, found one, took a step forward, then halted. Rayne was pushing through the doors of the station. She spotted him, faltered to a stop, then forced a bright smile onto her face. The obvious effort it cost her made Avery's spirits sink to an all-time low.

'Hello, handsome,' she said with equally forced brightness. 'I don't know about you, but I feel like I've been put through the wringer.' She grimaced.

Avery nodded. 'Ditto. I was thinking about breakfast,' he said, indicating the café across the road. 'Want to join me?'

How sad, he thought. After all we've been through, now we're talking like strangers.

'Sure,' Rayne said, with an obvious lack of enthusiasm. Together they crossed the road and entered the café. They ordered coffee and toast, neither quite knowing what to say next. So they sat in silence while the waitress deposited their food, then Avery began to butter a slice of toast and add a lacklustre dollop of marmalade.

Rayne sighed. 'The man on the train, it turns out, was called Felix Barstow. My PA back in England ID'd him. He was hired by Greg Nones, as we thought. Who, by the way, even as we speak, is sampling the hospitality of one of Her Majesty's prisons.' When Avery raised an eyebrow, she took a sip of coffee and shrugged. 'He was caught trying to leave the country. I'm sorry, Avery, but he'd rifled the company accounts.'

Avery sighed. He should, he supposed, be feeling a lot more angry than he was. It could set Cloud Nine back months. There'd be the lawyers to pay to sort it all out, not to mention the accountants. No doubt the tax man would come sniffing as well, scenting blood. But the truth was, none of it seemed important anymore.

'Our firm was keeping an eye on him, so at least he didn't get away with it,' Rayne carried on, stirring her coffee, although she hadn't put in any sugar. He was so quiet. So down. She felt guilty again, and fought back the urge to reach across to him, hold his hand, and tell him that everything would be all right. But she knew he wouldn't be interested in tea and sympathy from her. *Especially* from her. She was surprised he'd even invited her to have breakfast with him in the first place. He must be heartily sick of the sight of her. 'I'm sorry,' she mumbled wretchedly.

'Why?' he asked blankly. 'Like you said, if it hadn't been for you, Greg would be sunning himself in the Bahamas by now on Cloud Nine's money. Plus, I'd probably be dead.'

'I didn't mean that,' Rayne said, with a small, ineffably sad smile. 'I meant that I'm sorry for everything else. About being here. About thinking you were a crook. About investigating you. About lying to you, and tricking you.'

'Oh,' Avery said flatly. 'That.'

In truth, he hadn't really thought much about all that. He'd always known that Rayne Fletcher was no ordinary woman, so why apply the ordinary rules to her? But now that he did come to think about what she'd been up to, he couldn't help but grin. 'You did it really well,' he said admiringly. 'I never even guessed.'

To his utter amazement, instead of grinning back and saying something about Mata Hari having nothing on her, her beautiful blue eyes seemed to fill with tears. He gaped at her, then swallowed hard, as his world turned topsy-turvy. 'Rayne, what's wrong?' he asked urgently. As tears spilled down her cheeks, she fumbled for a napkin and wiped her eyes. 'Rayne, what's wrong?' he persisted. 'Don't cry. Please.' He didn't know what to do with a weeping Rayne Fletcher.

She sniffed and managed a shaky laugh. 'Sorry. It just caught me on the raw, that's all,' she said, her lower lip trembling as she began to compulsively tear the damp tissue into pieces. 'Usually it wouldn't matter,' she said, confusing him utterly. 'I'd be flattered if a mark complimented me on how good I was at my job. I was always a fabulous liar,' she carried on, matter-of-factly. 'But from you it . . .' Her eyes filled again and she snarled, 'Oh damn!' and sobbed into the dissolving tissue again.

Over at the counter, Avery was aware of the waitress staring at them, but he ignored her. Somewhere, deep inside himself, some kind of an alarm was going off, and for some really strange reason it seemed to be making him glad. Why it should, when the woman of his dreams was crying into her coffee and was about to fly out of his life for good, was a complete mystery.

He waited for a gap in her sobs, then reached out and touched her hand. 'What is it? What's up?' he said softly.

Rayne gave her eyes a final wipe and slumped, utterly defeated, back into her seat. She looked at him for a moment, his wonderful, familiar face, his concerned, beautiful eyes, and managed a hiccoughing sigh. 'Well, why not,' she said softly, almost as if to herself. 'You deserve to have the last laugh. The truth is, I fell for you, didn't I?' Her chin came up in a challenge, daring him, or perhaps willing him, to laugh.

Avery felt the chair he was sitting in give a massive jolt. In fact, it felt as if the whole room tilted. For a moment he thought it was an earthquake, then realized that, no, it wasn't. It was only him suffering from seismic shock.

'You . . . fell . . . for me,' he repeated, stringing out the words as if unable to believe them.

Rayne laughed. Her blonde curls were limp, her face strained. After a night spent in the police station, she'd never felt less attractive or less in control. 'Yeah. Ironic, huh?' She felt her lips curl into a humourless smile. 'The bitter bit, as my gran would have said. So, go on. You can laugh. I don't mind.'

But she did mind. She felt, in fact, as if her heart was breaking. 'I conned you, and all the time I was falling in love with you. Go on, have a good crow about it,' she said, crossing her arms defiantly across her breasts.

Avery blinked at her. 'You mean . . . it wasn't all an act?' he said, feeling a huge grin welling up somewhere inside him, even as he battled to make sense of this sudden, unbelievable, wonderful reversal of fortune. 'You weren't just pretending?'

Rayne stared at him. 'Of course it wasn't an act,' she said, a slow, red, angry flush tinting her face as her eyes narrowed dangerously. Then, with her voice rising in growing anger, she snarled, 'Or do you think I go to bed with all the lying, thieving little villains I investigate?'

Avery blinked again. 'Hey, wait a minute . . .'

Rayne shot to her feet. 'Of all the damned nerve. Of all the damned—'

'Shut up!' Avery roared. 'I'm the injured party here, remember?' he yelled, also getting to his feet. Together they faced each other across the café table, chins thrust out belligerently. Then Rayne slowly backed down. She flushed guiltily. She wasn't used to eating humble pie. Or crow. And she didn't particularly like the taste of either.

'Yeah, OK,' she agreed reluctantly.

Avery thought she looked adorable. In fact, she looked like the most beautiful girl in the world.

'You love me,' he said, smugly.

Rayne's eyes flashed. 'Of course I love you, you prat!' she hissed. 'Haven't I just been telling you so?' And bit back a sob. But what good would it do her now?

And suddenly, Avery understood. In an instant he saw it all, right there in the flash of fear in her eyes and the misery on her face. 'Oh, Rayne,' he groaned. 'You idiot. You saved my life. I loved you from the moment we met. Do you really think I care how or why we met? Yes, I've been miserable since I learned why you were here, but only because I thought it meant I'd lost you. That I was just another case for you, part of your job, and that I could now be filed away while you went on to something, and somebody, else.'

Rayne's eyes slowly widened. She stared at him. 'You're not having me on, are you?' she said at last. She didn't think she could take that — even if her critics, and she herself, might think deep down that she probably deserved it.

'Of course I'm not having you on,' Avery said helplessly. 'Can't you tell when a bloke's head over heels in love with you, for Pete's sake?'

Rayne's eyes began to shine, and her heart to swell. 'You mean it? You really love me?' she breathed.

Avery grinned at her. 'Of course I love you. You prat!'

And then she was in his arms, kissing him passionately, crawling all over him like a particularly tenacious rash as the wide-eyed waitress, from behind the safety of her counter, sighed loudly in approval.

* * *

In Perth, Persis walked down a hospital corridor and hesitated outside the door. A nurse walked by, looked at her and the man standing beside her with open curiosity, then went on her busy, bustling way.

Persis felt warm fingers slip into her own and turned to look at Dane. He smiled, his courage bolstering her own. 'Ready?' he asked softly, and she nodded. It was now or never.

Together they walked into the room.

Sunlight, bright and blue-tinged from Perth's coastal ambience, filtered into the room, illuminating the orchids and roses which filled several vases. But the presence of terminal illness was inescapable. White blinds swayed with the warm breeze coming through the open window, but all eyes were drawn inevitably to the bed — and the ancient woman, stick-thin but still somehow vital, who was lying on the mattress, attached to tubes and machines which blip-blipped unobtrusively.

The frail head, topped by sparse white curls, turned on the pillow, and Persis gasped as a pair of eyes as green as Dane's own suddenly bored into them. The old woman's face lit up as she recognized Dane, and Persis felt her heart nearly break with the pity and beauty of it.

Without a word, Dane walked forward, his hand reaching into the top of his shirt pocket. The green eyes, the only thing which seemed alive in that frail body, fastened onto the movement with an almost fanatical hope. The emotion was electric.

Dane slowly withdrew his hand, and the opal flashed its magnificent rainbow fire into the room.

Of course, Persis suddenly thought. *Iris*. Iris was the goddess of the rainbow. No wonder the Cartwrights had named the fabulous jewel after her.

The old woman sighed and made a noise. The nurses had already told them that she was incapable of speech after yet another minor stroke, although the sister believed that her patient had retained much of her former, remarkable intelligence. Persis had to agree with that assessment now, as she watched Dane place the stone tenderly into his grandmother's hand. For although it was true that he had to lift her hand from the bed for her, there was no mistaking the joy and sudden peace in her face, as she looked at the stone gleaming palely in her palm.

'I found it for you, Gran,' he said softly. 'It's back where it belongs.'

She made another noise. Although he couldn't possibly understand it, Dane seemed somehow to know exactly what she wanted.

'No, no trouble. And there'll be no scandal. Nobody will ever know. This . . .' He turned, and held out his hand to Persis, who went instantly to his side and slipped her hand into his. 'Is Persis Canfield-Hope.'

The eyes turned quickly to her and Persis felt herself tense. This woman, after all, had been Walter C's lawful wife. And Angela had been, in her eyes, forever the 'other woman'. The usurper. The one who had, humiliatingly, taken the Iris Stone away from her. How could she expect her to be pleased to meet the granddaughter of her arch-rival?

'This is the woman I love, Gran,' Dane continued calmly and firmly. 'The woman I've asked to marry me, and who has consented to be my wife.'

The green eyes flashed to Dane in obvious surprise. Something seemed to pass between the vibrant, strong, young man and the old, dying woman. For, slowly, the green eyes looked back to Persis with an obvious question in them.

Persis glanced at Dane, then back to the woman on the bed, then down at their hands entwined around the Iris Stone. Lifting her eyes once more to Dane's grandmother, she began to speak.

'I never knew my grandmother, Angela. She died during the Blitz. Last year, I was ill, and my mother found my grandmother's diaries and brought them to me when I was in hospital. I read them and found them fascinating. But I had no idea who Walter C was, or anything about the opal.' Her eyes dropped to the Iris Stone, which seemed to glow in mute satisfaction in the old lady's hand. 'I came to Australia only to recuperate in the sun, and to follow my grandmother's trek across Australia.'

The green eyes held steady on her face.

Persis took a breath and continued. 'I met Dane in Sydney. I had no idea who he was, only that he was special. And the more time we spent together, the more I came to realize that I loved him. Really loved him.'

Persis paused there, wishing she could say something else, something more emphatic, something which would make this woman know, without a doubt, how much Dane meant to her. It was imperative that she understood this. Then she felt Dane reach out with his other hand and grasp hers. And once again, it gave her the courage to go on.

'But as we got to know each other, I began to sense that there was something . . . holding him back,' she continued, her voice wavering just a little now. 'Something was wrong. And then, on the train to Kalgoorlie, I realized he'd been reading my grandmother's diary. And an even greater shock came when I found a letter in his cabin from Walter C. I realized then that it couldn't be a coincidence, us meeting the way we had. And I felt . . . well, quite frankly, I felt scared,' she admitted, meeting the old woman's eyes without flinching.

The green eyes left her face momentarily, went back to Dane's, then returned once more to her. Was it her imagination, or did they seem softer? Persis took another breath, and went on.

'I didn't know what was going on. From the diary, I thought my grandmother might have had an illegitimate child, a daughter called Iris. I wasn't sure what Dane wanted from the diary, but I knew it was imperative that I find out. If we were to have any chance of a life together,' she explained, looking at Dane with all the love and longing plain to see on her beautiful face, 'then I had to find out what was standing between us and deal with it.'

She smiled as he looked back at her, steadily, adoringly, the love he felt for her as plain to see on his own strong, masculine features.

'And so, in Kalgoorlie I did some research,' she continued. 'And clues in the diary and from the letter led me to an old mine. It was called the Sweetheart Mine. And it was there I found it,' she said simply, looking down at the opal.

'I followed her there,' Dane said, taking up the story. 'When I saw her with the opal, I thought she must have known about it all along. It was the worst moment of my life,' he said simply, his voice deepening with remembered pain.

He looked down at his grandmother, who'd made a small, sympathetic sound, and smiled grimly. 'So I demanded it back. I accused her of being just like her grandmother — of being out to get what she could. Of reclaiming something which had never belonged to the Canfield-Hopes in the first place.'

He paused, then looked back at Persis, each of them remembering those fraught few minutes back in the mine. His sudden appearance had scared her, but his harsh words afterwards had scared her even more.

'But I didn't understand what he was talking about,' Persis said softly. 'When he came and took the opal from my hand, I still didn't realise that it was the stone which had been standing between us all this time.'

'And when she did, she didn't want it, Gran,' Dane said, the wonderment, relief and love in his voice coming across as strongly now as it had back in the Sweetheart Mine, when Persis had first told him as much, and he'd admitted his love for her was, and always had been, real.

'It's very beautiful, of course,' Persis said, looking down at the Iris Stone now. 'But it's not important,' she said. Then added hastily, in case the old woman should think it was some sort of criticism of her, 'I mean, not to *me*, anyway. Not to *us* — the Canfield-Hope family. My mother never even knew of it — none of us did. My grandmother, after all, never even brought it back to England.'

'We don't think she ever meant to,' Dane said. 'We think Grandpa gave it to her sometime before taking her down into the mine. By that time, according to her diary, she knew she was going to have to return home, because of the threat of war.'

'We're pretty sure that she dug a hole in the beam of the mine, where she knew it was damp and the moist air would keep the stone from drying out, and hid it there,' Persis continued, holding the old lady's gaze firmly now. 'There was a line in her diary about her not being able to accept some fabulous gift he'd given her. I think she meant to tell him where it was after she'd returned home. But either she died before she could, or the letter went astray — it was wartime, after all — and Walter never knew.'

The old lady sighed heavily, and Dane lifted her other hand to his lips and kissed it briefly. Then he held out his arm to Persis, who moved to stand within its protective circle eagerly.

Together, they watched the old woman anxiously.

'I love her, Gran,' he said simply. 'And she loves me.'

And, on the bed, the old lady seemed to understand what he was asking. Her eyes went from the stone, to Persis, then back to the stone. Slowly, carefully, ready to stop if at any moment he realized he'd read her intentions wrongly, Dane lifted the stone from his grandmother's hand.

The green eyes, so like his own, went straight to Persis. Slowly, Dane undid the clasp, reached up, and began to drape the necklace around Persis's throat. Instinctively, Persis reached up to stop him. 'No, you don't have to. I told you, it's not—'

'Shussh,' Dane said softly. 'She's giving us her blessing. Let her.'

Persis blinked back sudden tears, then nodded. She swallowed painfully and when he lowered his hand, the Iris Stone flashed rainbow colours from just above her left breast.

'I love you,' she said softly.

Dane reached up and ran his finger lightly across the line of her jaw. 'Even though I doubted you? Right to the end?'

Persis nodded. 'Even so,' she said softly. After all, what was love without forgiveness? How long could passion last if there was no understanding? What use was a proposal of marriage if they didn't understand the concept of compromise?

And what chance did any marriage have if neither partner was prepared to mean it when they said for better or for worse?

'As long as you're sure now,' she warned softly, 'and never doubt me again.'

Slowly he leaned forward and kissed her.

'Never again,' he promised.

From the bed the old lady watched them and sighed peacefully. And the Iris Stone, catching a stray beam of sunlight after sixty years encased in darkness, flashed a celebratory rainbow of colour into the air — beautiful and opalescent.

THE END

ALSO BY FAITH MARTIN

DI HILLARY GREENE SERIES
Book 1: MURDER ON THE OXFORD CANAL
Book 2: MURDER AT THE UNIVERSITY
Book 3: MURDER OF THE BRIDE
Book 4: MURDER IN THE VILLAGE
Book 5: MURDER IN THE FAMILY
Book 6: MURDER AT HOME
Book 7: MURDER IN THE MEADOW
Book 8: MURDER IN THE MANSION
Book 9: MURDER IN THE GARDEN
Book 10: MURDER BY FIRE
Book 11: MURDER AT WORK
Book 12: MURDER NEVER RETIRES
Book 13: MURDER OF A LOVER
Book 14: MURDER NEVER MISSES
Book 15: MURDER AT MIDNIGHT
Book 16: MURDER IN MIND
Book 17: HILLARY'S FINAL CASE
Book 18: HILLARY'S BACK

JENNY STARLING MYSTERIES
Book 1: THE BIRTHDAY MYSTERY
Book 2: THE WINTER MYSTERY
Book 3: THE RIVERBOAT MYSTERY
Book 4: THE CASTLE MYSTERY
Book 5: THE OXFORD MYSTERY
Book 6: THE TEATIME MYSTERY
Book 7: THE COUNTRY INN MYSTERY

MONICA NOBLE MYSTERIES
Book 1: THE VICARAGE MURDER
Book 2: THE FLOWER SHOW MURDER
Book 3: THE MANOR HOUSE MURDER

GREAT READS

THE LYING GAME
AN OXFORD REVENGE
AN OXFORD SCANDAL
AN OXFORD ENEMY
AN OXFORD SECRET
AN OXFORD FRAUD
AN OXFORD TRIAL
AN OXFORD INHERITANCE
AN OXFORD SUSPECT
IMPOSTERS IN PARADISE
HEART OF FIRE
HIDDEN RAINBOWS

Thank you for reading this book.

If you enjoyed it please leave feedback on Amazon or Goodreads, and if there is anything we missed or you have a question about, then please get in touch. We appreciate you choosing our book.

Founded in 2014 in Shoreditch, London, we at Joffe Books pride ourselves on our history of innovative publishing. We were thrilled to be shortlisted for Independent Publisher of the Year at the British Book Awards.

www.joffebooks.com

We're very grateful to eagle-eyed readers who take the time to contact us. Please send any errors you find to corrections@joffebooks.com. We'll get them fixed ASAP.